Husband

A Marriage of Convenience Romance
A Keeper Series, Book 4

MELISSA McCLONE

The Husband: A Marriage of Convenience Romance
A Keeper Series (Book 4)
Copyright © 2020 Melissa McClone
Second Edition

Previously published as *Marriage for Baby*.

Cover by EmCat Designs

Cardinal Press, LLC
July 2020
ISBN-13: 9781944777524

Other Books by Melissa McClone

All series stories are standalone,
but past characters may reappear.

One Night to Forever Series

Can one night change your life…
and your relationship status?
Fiancé for the Night
The Wedding Lullaby
A Little Bit Engaged
Love on the Slopes
The One Night To Forever Box Set: Books 1-4

The Billionaires of Silicon Forest

Who will be the last single man standing?
The Wife Finder
The Wish Maker
The Deal Breaker

Mountain Rescue Series

Finding love in Hood Hamlet
with a little help from Christmas magic…
His Christmas Wish
Her Christmas Secret
Her Christmas Kiss
His Second Chance
His Christmas Family

A Keeper Series
These men know what they want, and love isn't on their
list. But what happens when each meets a keeper?
The Groom
The Soccer Star
The Boss
The Husband

For the complete list of books, go to:
melissamcclone.com/books.com

Dedication

For Virginia Kantra and Tiffany Talbott,
talented writers and friends extraordinaire.

Special thanks to Ceci and Robert Kramer.

Chapter One

Kate Malone didn't want to be in Idaho. She should be in Portland, Oregon, about to attend a meeting or take a call. But life could change in an instant.

Or be lost in one.

On the sidewalk outside the law office in Boise, she stared at the double glass doors. Every nerve ending twitched with a sense of dread.

Go inside.

She should.

Instead, Kate glanced at her cell phone before blowing out a relieved breath. Her appointment didn't start for a few minutes.

Good. No reason to rush because she wanted to pretend for a little while longer this was all a big mistake. A misunderstanding. Anything so it wouldn't be real.

If only that were the case…

She raised her face to the cloudless, blue sky. The spring sunshine heated her cheeks. Sun kisses. That was what Susan called them.

Susan.

The unusually warm April day reminded Kate of their college graduation nine years ago. She'd approached the proceedings as a necessary step, one more item to mark off her to-do list on the way to the top, but not her best friend. Susan had relished each moment of the drawn-out ceremony in the sweltering ninety-degree heat. She'd bounced across the stage, tossed her University of Oregon diploma box in the air, and twirled around.

Twice.

A smile tugged on Kate's lips. Susan always lived life to the fullest. Or rather…

Had lived.

Until a driver fell asleep at the wheel and collided head-on with Susan's car two days ago here in Boise.

As grief slashed through Kate, her breath hitched. Tears stung her eyes.

How could Susan be dead?

Susan, so full of life, so full of love. Susan, with her adoring husband, Brady, and their cute baby, Cassidy…

All three had died in the crash.

Kate swallowed hard.

No. She wasn't losing control now.

She didn't have a tissue.

Or the time.

She needed to hold herself together during the meeting with Susan and Brady's attorney. Once Kate checked into her hotel, she would fall apart but not until then.

Squaring her shoulders, she pushed open a door and stepped inside. As a blast of cold air hit her, goose bumps prickled on her arms. The sight of the empty receptionist desk deflated her resolve. Her composure slipped a notch. Now that she was here, she wanted this over.

"Kate?"

The familiar male voice made her stiffen.

Jared.

Oh, no. She wasn't ready to face him. Not now. Possibly not ever. And yet she turned toward his voice.

As Jared rose from a leather club chair, her breath caught in her throat. He wore a tailored gray suit and the multicolored silk tie she'd given him for his twenty-ninth birthday.

Four years ago, when Brady and Susan introduced them, Jared Reed had been a twenty-five-year-old single woman's fantasy. Kate thought he was younger, but her being older than him hadn't mattered. She'd fallen head over heels instantly.

He still looked younger than he was. He was also more handsome.

Her heart thudded. She wished she still didn't find him so attractive.

His square jaw, slightly crooked nose—from a snowboarding accident when he was a teenager—and light brown beard gave his face the right amount of rugged character to offset his long lashes and lush lips. His hair had grown longer in the last three months. He usually wore a short, corporate cut, but the wavy, carefree style suited him better.

Not that she cared.

Much.

His hazel-green eyes met hers. "How are you?"

"I-I'm—" Her voice cracked. Tears blurred her vision.

No. Kate didn't want him to see her like this.

She blinked. Once, twice.

"I'm so sorry, Katie." He was at her side in an instant and brushed his lips across her forehead. "So very sorry."

At the best of times, she struggled to remain indifferent to him, but his tender gesture and simple, yet sincere, words shattered her defenses. She sunk against him, breathing in his familiar soap and water scent, drawing in the welcome comfort of his hard chest.

Stop...now, logic shouted.

Move away...now, common sense cried.

Kate didn't want to listen. She didn't care if her actions contradicted rational thought. Jared understood what she was going through. He was experiencing the same grief.

"I'm sorry, too," she choked out. "It's so..."

He wrapped his arms around her. "Horrible."

She hugged him, not wanting to let go. "I keep hoping it's a mistake, or I'll wake up to find out it's been a bad dream."

"Me, too," he admitted. "As soon as I heard, I called your office. They said you were out of town."

"Boston."

"I didn't want to leave a message."

"I wouldn't have gotten it." She closed her eyes. Not being alone felt so good. "After my assistant called me with the news, I turned off my phone."

"A first."

"I hope I never have to do it again."

He gave her shoulder a reassuring squeeze. "So do I."

She stared at him. "I'm sorry I didn't call you."

"You wouldn't have been able to reach me. I was in San Francisco. My boss had me pulled out of a meeting and relayed the message." A corner of Jared's mouth lifted. "Besides, I didn't expect you to call, Kate."

She flinched. "Why not? Brady was your best friend."

"Susan was like a sister to you. How old were you when you met?"

"Seven." In a foster home. Kate's first. Susan's third. That had been so long ago. They had come so far.

"Seven," he repeated. "You must be devastated."

Devastated didn't begin to describe the anguish ripping Kate apart. It was as if a part of her had died, too. She inhaled slowly.

Jared's arms tightened around her, and she rested her head against his chest, a foreign yet familiar position. "It's okay to cry, Katie."

The urge to pull away was strong. She fought it because she didn't want to step back. Not when she relished the steady beat of his heart beneath her cheek. It was what she needed.

"I've cried." Kate tried not to sound defensive, but she had cried. More than she cared to admit. She just didn't like crying in front of others.

"I spoke to Brady last week," Jared said. "Susan e-mailed me a picture of Cassidy on Thursday. She promised to send more."

But those pictures would never arrive. The baby girl would grow no bigger.

Kate smothered a sob. "I can't believe they're gone. Why them? Why now?"

"I wish I knew."

"Me, too."

But thinking about what she'd lost hurt so much. Too much. She would rather focus on something else. Someone else.

Jared.

Kate curled the ends of his hair with her finger. It had never been long enough to do this before, and she liked the extra length.

He brushed his hand through her hair, his fingers sifting through the blond strands, the way he always had.

She nearly sighed.

It was as if nothing had changed between them. That was far from the truth, but Kate wasn't ready to back out of his arms.

For now, she would pretend the past didn't matter and ignore the future. She could do that because she needed Jared—his warmth, his strength, him. A part of her hoped he needed her, too.

At least for a little while.

He cupped her face with his left hand—a thick gold band on his ring finger.

Hers felt conspicuously bare. She curled her left hand into a fist.

"Mr. and Mrs. Reed?" a female voice asked.

Jared turned his head. "Yes?"

A cute brunette with short, curly hair, and dangling gold earrings stood next to the receptionist's desk.

Kate backed out of his embrace. "Actually, I'm—"

"My wife. Kate Malone," he interrupted, a slight edge to his voice. "I'm Jared Reed."

Kate recalled the long discussions about her not taking his name when they'd gotten engaged. He'd claimed to understand, to accept her decision. But he hadn't. Not really.

She shifted uncomfortably.

"I'm sorry, Ms. Malone. Mr. Reed." The woman picked up a thick manila file from the receptionist's desk. "Don Phillips is running a few minutes late. I'll show you to his office once I drop off this folder."

"Thank you," Jared said.

As the woman walked away, Kate bit her lip. "Why didn't you tell her the truth?"

"Because with or without your wedding ring, you're still my wife." His gaze hardened. "At least until the divorce is finalized."

Chapter Two

The receptionist led them down a hallway and motioned to an open door at the end. "Don will be right with you."

"Thanks." Jared hoped the atmosphere in the office would be more comfortable than that of the lobby. But knowing Kate, he wouldn't hold his breath.

The woman smiled. "Let me know if you need anything."

"We will." He fought the temptation to ask the friendly receptionist to stay until the lawyer joined them because her presence might ease the tension between him and Kate. Not to mention the silence. She hadn't spoken to him since he'd said divorce.

His jaw clamped.

Maybe she'd forgotten she was the one who filed.

No. That wasn't fair.

She'd lost her best friend and goddaughter. She was in tremendous pain.

Kate sat in a chair in front of a large mahogany desk. With posture that would make a charm school proud, she appeared poised and in control as she studied the diploma hanging on the wall. Not surprising. She kept her emotions under a tight lid and hated showing any sign of weakness.

Or at least until she entered the law office on the verge of tears. She had looked so lost and alone. Her sadness had clawed at his heart.

Jared sat in the chair next to her and extended his hand. "You okay?"

She nodded once, not meeting his gaze. Maybe she didn't see his hand, either.

He'd tried.

No one could say he hadn't tried to save his marriage or hadn't wanted to give the relationship another go.

He had, and he would.

If she gave him a chance.

Ironic. Brady and Susan had introduced him to Kate. Now their deaths were bringing them back together.

The seconds turned into minutes.

The only sound was the ticking of a vintage Felix the Cat clock. One thing hadn't changed since the last time he saw Kate—the same stone-cold silence. Three months ago, they'd been in Boise for Cassidy's baptism. The weekend hadn't gone well. Separation and divorce had come up, but he hadn't expected the call from Kate's lawyer the next week. Now, lawyers handled the communication between them. That was strange.

Wrong.

Yet, she wouldn't consider another option.

He brushed his hand through his hair. "Kate—"

"There's a reason I'm not wearing my wedding rings."

Uh-oh. Jared drew a cautious breath. With emotions running high, words and actions could easily be misconstrued. They were hurting enough, but he couldn't deny how seeing her ringless finger had affected him. "You don't owe me any explanations."

"I was afraid the ring might fall off," she said anyway, still not meeting his eyes. "I lost some weight."

More than "some," given how she'd felt in his arms—thinner and fragile.

He'd chalked it up to grief. Now, he wasn't so sure.

Kate never left the house without looking perfect—hair, makeup, clothing. She called it the "whole package," even though she was as beautiful to him in ratty old sweats, a stained T-shirt, and a ponytail.

Today, however, Kate appeared as if she'd had to work harder on her image. The energetic, multitasking dynamo, who owned one of the hottest and fastest-growing public relations firms in the Pacific Northwest, had all but disappeared.

Jared expected Kate's blue eyes to be red and swollen, given the circumstances, but not so wary, stressed, exhausted. Her sunken cheeks and loose-fitting designer clothes went beyond grief, and the changes worried him.

"You need to remember to eat," he said.

"I eat."

He raised an eyebrow.

She set her chin. "I forget sometimes."

Most of the time. Jared used to text her at lunchtime and dinnertime. Now that he wasn't around to remind her, she probably didn't bother with decent meals. "You should schedule food into your day."

"I do," she said, a little too quickly. "Do you?"

"I don't need to. I enjoy food too much to skip meals."

"I don't skip meals. I forget." Her mouth twitched. "I don't want to argue."

She never did. The only place Kate lost control was in bed. "We're not arguing."

"Just drop it. Okay?"

He checked the time. The second hand moved slower than his niece's turtle, Corky.

"Sorry to keep you waiting." A middle-aged man,

wearing a tailored navy suit and wire-rimmed glasses, burst into the office. "I'm Don Phillips, the Lukases' attorney."

Jared rose and shook the man's hand. "Jared Reed."

Kate remained seated. "Kate Malone."

The lawyer sat behind his desk, and Jared sat, too.

"I'm sorry for the loss of your friends," Don said. "It's such a tragedy."

Jared nodded.

Kate placed her clasped hands on her lap.

"Thank you for coming so quickly." Don reached for a file. "I'd hoped to speak with you when I called, but under the circumstances, it was imperative to get you to Boise as soon as possible."

"We understand," Jared said. "Have funeral arrangements been made?"

"Yes." Don pulled out a piece of paper from the file. "Mr. Lukas, Brady's father, took care of that. The funeral home is holding a vigil on Wednesday and a memorial service on Thursday. The church will host a reception in the hall afterward. Then, the bodies will be flown to Maine for burial."

The lawyer made it sound so easy, as if he were reading a checklist.

"Susan..." Kate's voice trailed off.

"What?" Jared asked.

"It's just"—she tucked her hair behind her ears— "Susan never really liked Maine."

13

"No, she didn't," Don agreed. "But she and Brady put their burial location in their wills."

"Oh." Kate wet her lips. "Okay, then."

"A situation like this is never easy, but fortunately, Brady and Susan had the foresight to plan for such an occurrence."

Occurrence?

A chill inched along Jared's spine. Perhaps that was legalese for death. Either way, the words were difficult for him to hear.

"No amount of planning will make this easier to deal with, but logistically, having wills in place help things proceed a little smoother." Don pulled out a thick document from the file. "I attended the same church as Brady and Susan, and I drew up their wills. Since they had no family in town, I kept the originals here in the office."

"Shouldn't we wait for Brady's parents?" Jared asked.

"Mr. and Mrs. Lukas aren't coming," Don explained. "Although Mr. Lukas handled the funeral arrangements, their doctors said the trip from the East Coast would be too much for them with their current health conditions. After the wills were written, Brady's parents received copies of both, so they know and agree with what their son and daughter-in-law decided. May I proceed?"

Jared nodded. But he thought hearing this must tear Kate up inside. He watched for her reaction, but she held herself together tightly, so he ignored the urge to touch her.

"As you know, Brady was an only child, and Susan had been in foster homes since she was five. They had no living relatives other than Brady's parents." Don's gaze rested on Kate. "Though Susan considered you more a sister than a friend."

Kate's composed facade cracked for an instant. "It was the same for me."

"The Lukases thought highly of you, Jared," Don said. "Brady and Susan each named you their personal representative to handle their estates. Do you accept their nominations?"

Jared didn't know what sort of responsibilities would be involved as Brady and Susan's executor, but that didn't matter. "I'm honored and happy to accept. May I retain your services? I've never done this before, so I'll need your expertise."

"I'll gladly counsel and offer my assistance. The sooner we get started, the better. I would like to submit the wills and obtain your appointment as their personal representative through informal proceedings. That way, a hearing won't be required."

Proceedings. Hearing.

Jared's muscles tensed. A few weeks ago, he'd been making plans to attend a poker tournament with Brady while Kate spent the weekend with Susan. Now he was overseeing their friends' probate.

As Don scribbled notes on a yellow legal pad,

Jared glanced at Kate. She acted like this was nothing more than another one of the endless meetings she attended, but her hands trembled. He wanted to pull her onto his lap and hold her until she smiled again.

"Once you're officially appointed their personal representative, you'll want to call a locksmith and have the locks changed on the Lukases's residence," Don said. "I can provide recommendations."

"I'd appreciate the referrals," Jared said.

"Why change the locks?" Kate asked.

"We don't know who might have keys to the house," Don explained. "Babysitters, neighbors, housecleaners. The list goes on. You don't want to chance a robbery. Unfortunately, such break-ins have occurred in situations like this."

Jared recalled the two-story house Brady and Susan called home. The couple had been too busy working on the nursery to fix up the rest of the house. Now that task would fall to the new owner. Jared pictured his and Kate's home, and the hours they'd spent working on the old house. Kate obsessing over paint chips. Kissing on a ladder. Making love on a drop cloth. That seemed so long ago.

Soon the house would be hers.

He hadn't fought Kate for it, even though he loved the home, with all its creaks, quirks, and inadequate plumbing. But his life was no longer in Portland or with Kate. Even though the words never seemed to make things easier, he kept telling himself that.

"Do I have your permission to proceed?" Don asked.

"Please do," Jared said, grateful for the lawyer's help.

Don shuffled papers. "And now, Cassidy."

Kate's befuddlement matched Jared's confusion.

"What about Cassidy?" he asked.

"You and Kate have been nominated for joint guardianship in both wills," Don said, but his words made no sense. "You realize, of course, you are under no legal obligation to accept the guardian appointment."

Kate's lower lip quivered. "I don't understand."

Neither did Jared. Guardian? Of Cassidy? But... "There has to be some mistake."

"I suggest clients discuss guardianship with prospective nominees before naming them in their wills," Don added. "Otherwise, the nomination can come as a shock."

Shock didn't come close. Jared shook his head. "You don't understand—"

"They discussed it with us." Kate's voice sounded hoarse, unnatural. "But Cassidy is dead."

The lawyer frowned.

Jared reached for her hand and laced his fingers with hers. "The message I received said the family had been in an accident, and the Lukases were dead."

"I was told the same," Kate said.

"Oh, no. There's been a miscommunication."

Don's expression turned grim. "Cassidy was in the accident, but she survived."

Kate's mouth dropped open. She clung to Jared's hand.

He understood the roller coaster of emotions—afraid to hope, afraid to believe because the letdown would be even worse.

"She's alive?" Kate whispered.

Jared held his breath.

"Cassidy is very much alive." Don set his pen on the desk. "She's at the hospital recovering from her injuries."

An enormous weight lifted from Jared's shoulders. Brady loved his baby girl, but he would have wanted her to go on with or without him.

Kate jumped up from her chair, pulling Jared with her.

Tears streamed down her face. As she smiled at him, an almost forgotten warmth seeped into his heart. "I can't believe it."

He smiled back. "Believe it."

She hugged him. The scent of her shampoo—grapefruit—tickled his nose. Her mane of hair brushed against him, and he remembered how much he'd missed holding her and touching her and loving her.

"Is it wrong to be happy?" she whispered, her warm breath caressing his neck.

"It's fine, Kate." Jared held on to her. "I feel the same way."

They both laughed, a sound he never thought he'd hear in the future, let alone today.

"I'm so sorry." Don removed his glasses and rubbed his eyes. "It was a difficult day. I thought I was clear on the phone, but perhaps I wasn't."

"Cassidy's alive." Kate sat, but she didn't let go of Jared's hand, so he sat, too. "That's what matters. Is she okay?"

"Cassidy is in stable condition," Don explained. "The car seat protected her from more serious injuries."

Kate sucked in a breath.

Jared blew his out.

"What?" Don asked.

"Our baby shower gift was the car seat," Jared said.

Don leaned forward. "An excellent present for new parents."

Jared nodded. Kate had spent hours poring over catalogs and reading car seat reviews in order to pick the right one. He'd called her out for being obsessive again, but her research had saved the baby's life.

Her lips parted. Was she remembering?

How could she not? Cassidy was alive. Her parents were dead. And the little girl belonged to him and Kate.

Jared remembered when Brady and Susan had flown to Portland for a weekend. Susan and Kate had spent the day shopping for maternity clothes while

Brady helped Jared build a trellis for the yard. That night over a bottle of sparkling cider, Brady and Susan asked them to be the baby's guardians. They told them to discuss the request and take their time if they needed it. Jared and Kate talked it over and agreed the next morning.

But that was before. Before the separation. Before Kate had filed for divorce.

"How recent is the will?" Jared asked.

"I met with Brady and Susan a week after Cassidy was born." Don got a faraway look in his eyes. "I remember them telling me this was the baby's first outing since coming home from the hospital. Susan said she'd put it into the baby book."

That made no sense. Brady and Susan would have known about the marriage problems, about Jared living and working in Seattle and Kate staying in Portland. Something didn't add up.

"What's the problem?" Kate asked. "We told them we would do it."

"This is a life-changing decision," Don said. "Don't rush. You have thirty days after we start guardianship proceedings to accept the appointment."

"We're not declining," she said.

Jared agreed with her. Of course he did. But he needed to be sure this was what his friends wanted for their daughter. Guardians with a disintegrating, soon-to-be-over marriage didn't seem like the number one choice parents would make. "Could you please read the guardianship portion of the will?"

Don paged through the paperwork. "Since Brady and Susan wanted to name both of you as guardians, I suggested additional wording to the wills, which they agreed to."

That made sense to Jared, and he wanted to hear what was written. Especially since Brady and Susan knew about the marriage problems.

"Here's the passage from Brady's will. Susan's is identical." The lawyer put on his glasses. "'If my spouse does not survive me and if at the time of my death any of my children are minors or under a legal disability, I appoint Jared Reed and Kate Malone to act jointly as the guardians of each child who is a minor or under a legal disability so long as Jared Reed and Kate Malone are both then living and married on the date of such appointment.'"

Kate straightened in her chair.

Her tension was palpable, but she shouldn't worry. They were living, and they were also still married. Everything would be fine.

At least as far as the baby was concerned.

Of course, Cassidy would become part of the divorce settlement. Susan would want Kate to have custody.

"Is there a provision if our marriage ends at a future date?" Kate asked, her voice cool.

"Actually, there is. Again, both wills contain the same wording." Don flipped the page. "'If Jared Reed and Kate Malone are not married to each other on the date of such appointment or become separated or divorced at a later date, I appoint Jared Reed to solely act as the guardian of each child of mine who is a minor or under a legal disability.'"

Kate's jaw dropped. "What?"

Jared sat, stunned. "Me?"

Chapter Three

Kate's heart pounded. Every muscle tensed. She didn't believe her ears.

She couldn't.

"There must be some mistake." Her gaze darted between a shell-shocked Jared and a contemplative Don. "Susan would never have agreed to that."

"It's not a mistake," Don said matter-of-factly as if they were discussing the custody of a pampered pet, not Kate's precious goddaughter. "Brady and Susan were clear with their wishes and made sure I understood them."

Kate flexed her fingers, fighting to grasp the situation. Fighting for control. "But it makes no sense."

"I agree." Jared's confident voice reassured her. "I

may have been nominated as the personal representative, but the sole guardian? Kate and Susan were as close as sisters. There's no reason I should be the one named in the wills."

Relief and gratitude washed over Kate. Thank goodness he understood how ridiculous this was. No doubt Jared would support her in getting this overturned.

His gaze met hers. They were on the same side for once. And that felt...good. Satisfying. In a way it hadn't for a very long time.

"Remember, that's only if you and Kate divorce," Don added. "As long as you are together, the provision doesn't apply."

Her relief ebbed.

The split of assets had been agreed upon; the paperwork had been filed. It was only a matter of time, weeks really, until the divorce was official.

Panic threatened. Kate grabbed on to the chair. She couldn't lose control.

Not when she had to think. Kate needed to figure out a way to fix this. First, they had to be named guardians. Together. Then she and Jared could challenge the validity of the will so she could gain sole guardianship of Cassidy. Of course, Jared would have whatever visitation rights he wanted.

She eased her death grip on the chair arms. Now that she had a plan formulated, she could cope.

"If it's any consolation, Kate," Don said, his voice

startling her, "you are named sole guardian if Jared dies."

"Don't give her any ideas."

His wry humor reminded Kate of the time he playfully accused her of poisoning him when she made juice using organic kale, rhubarb, and strawberries after a trip to the farmer's market.

A smile pulled at her mouth.

She caught herself. This wasn't the time for fun. She pressed her lips together.

"What happens next?" Jared asked the lawyer.

"Well, since you're married, you will both receive guardianship if you accept the nomination," Don explained. "But I'm sure this is something you want to discuss in private. No guardian can be named until the personal representative is officially appointed and the wills submitted for probate."

She struggled to make sense of his words, to understand their implications. "What about Cassidy? What happens to her in the meantime?"

"Cassidy is currently under state custody," Don said.

That was one thing Kate understood all too well. "No. Susan would not have wanted that for her baby."

"But since Cassidy's in the hospital, she won't be put into a foster home, correct?" Jared asked.

"Yes, as long as guardianship has been determined by the day of her release," Don said. "If we run into any snags, we can petition to have a temporary guardian named until final guardianship is determined."

Jared covered Kate's hand with his. "We'll make sure there aren't any snags."

She fought the urge to hug him. With everything they'd been through these past months, she'd forgotten Jared Reed was still a good guy. His reassurance meant so much.

Kate stole a glance at him, and he winked. Her pulse quickened. She mouthed the word *thanks* and looked away, as fast as she could without seeming rude. Gratefulness. That was all her reaction was, all it ever could be.

"Susan and Brady left letters for you." Don handed Kate a large, thick manila envelope, and Jared received a thin, standard business-size one. "Would you like to read them now or later?"

She clutched the envelope as if it were a winning Powerball lottery ticket. A part of her was afraid to look inside, but the other part wanted to rip the flap off and start reading. "Now."

"Later," Jared said at the same time.

Deadlock. They never could agree on anything. At first, their differences had been a joke, and they'd laughed about it. Over and over again. But their disagreements had been a sign. Even though she might have loved Jared, even though she might sometimes long for him, they didn't work well together.

"You can open yours later," she said. "I'd prefer to open mine now."

Jared ran his finger under the flap of the envelope. "Now is fine."

Don rose from the desk. "I'll get the paperwork started."

Kate mumbled a *thank you*. As she focused on the envelope in her hand, she heard paper crinkle and unfold and then a chuckle.

With trembling fingers, she opened the manila envelope and pulled out several typed pages.

Dear Kate,

If you're reading this, I'm dead, and it's a good thing I decided to write everything down for you. Brady thinks I'm being morbid, but until I had Cassidy, I didn't give much thought to what would happen if I weren't here. And now in the middle of all this estate planning, I've been thinking about it too much.

The corners of Kate's mouth curved. That was so like Susan. She thought about things too much. As did Kate. Obsessive? Perhaps. But she and Susan had called it analytical thinking.

By now, Don Phillips has told you that we want you and Jared to raise Cassidy. This should come as no surprise. What would come as a shock is if Don told you that Jared would gain custody of Cassidy if the two of you divorced. I know you're confused and mad at me.

Kate wasn't mad. How about stunned? Hurt? Bewildered? Betrayed? Her gaze strayed to Jared before returning to the letter.

My hope is you and Jared have resolved things before our untimely and unfortunate demise (gotta love that phrase!) and are living happily ever after. You are truly meant for each other.

Oh, Susan. She was such an optimist. Even under the most horrible situations growing up, she'd never stopped believing her life would improve. No matter what the odds. But this dream of Susan's wasn't in the cards for Kate.

And that realization hurt. Badly.

She'd wanted a family with Jared, but the timing always seemed wrong. They spent so little time together with their jobs. He wanted her to have a baby right when her company took off. And then he asked her to give up everything she'd put her heart and soul into and move to Seattle. When she wouldn't do what he wanted, he left without her.

Kate squeezed her eyes shut, but that didn't stop the memories or erase the pain.

"Here," Jared said.

She opened her eyes. He held out a tissue to her. She wasn't sure if his offer was out of compassion or pity. She didn't want him to think she was weak. Kate stiffened. "I don't need it."

"Just in case."

His half smile unfurled warmth inside her. And made her feel like an idiot. Jared was only trying to help her, not point out her weaknesses. She had to stop thinking of him as the enemy. Kate took the tissue. "Thank you."

"You're welcome."

His dark eyes seemed to see right through her, to her secret thoughts and feelings.

Heat. Fire. Passion.

Kate forced herself to breathe.

Okay, some sort of volatile chemistry remained between them. She'd go so far as to admit her physical attraction to Jared had increased during their separation.

No big deal.

A marriage couldn't survive on desire alone. She'd learned that lesson. She looked away.

"Are you finished?" Jared asked.

"No."

"I've read mine three times."

Did the letter mention her?

Old inadequacies floated to the surface. Had Brady questioned her ability to care for Cassidy?

Kate bit the inside of her cheek.

"What did the letter say?" she asked.

Jared smiled. "Typical Brady stuff, if that helps."

"I'm glad." She only hoped hers helped, too. Up until now, Susan's letter hadn't. "I need to finish mine."

"Go ahead."

Kate read how proud Susan was over Kate's accomplishments, their friendship, and their love for one another. As she continued, the paper shook and Kate realized her hands were trembling.

You and I know family doesn't have to mean blood relations, and that's what I'm counting on because I want Cassidy to experience what being part of a loving family is all about. Jared with the crazy, meddlesome Reeds can provide that for her. She can have what we didn't have growing up. I need that for my child.

As tears streamed from her eyes, she struggled to read the rest. She didn't like what Susan had written, but Kate understood and somehow that hurt more. Each word felt like a wound to her already aching heart. She fumbled for the tissue.

Jared handed her another one. She muttered thanks and wiped her eyes.

So much for challenging the will. She couldn't. Not when she knew what Susan wanted for her daughter. Kate would want the same for her own child. Wasn't that one reason she found Jared Reed with his large, supportive family so attractive when they'd first met? He'd had everything she hadn't had growing up.

But knowing the reasons and understanding them didn't make the circumstances any easier on her.

"Katie?" Jared placed his hand on her shoulder.

The warmth of his touch nearly did her in, but she couldn't—didn't want to—pull away.

He and Cassidy were all Kate had left.

She dabbed her eyes with a tissue again. "I'm not finished."

Forgive me if I've written something that has hurt you. I'm only doing what I feel is best for my daughter. I love you, Katie. I always have and I always will.

Take care of my baby and love her the way we wanted to be loved!

Hugs and love,

Susan

Kate didn't want to let Susan down, but that kind of love, the kind you didn't have to earn, wasn't possible. Not any longer. But for her best friend, Kate would give it her all.

She traced Susan's name—the only word handwritten on the many pages—with her fingertip. Tears dropped onto the paper, and Kate dried them off. She didn't want the letter to be ruined. She wanted to keep it.

For herself.

For Cassidy.

Kate inhaled and exhaled slowly. Steady. Calm. In control. She squared her shoulders. With a steady gaze, she met Jared's inquisitive eyes. "They want you to have Cassidy."

"I know."

Kate didn't want to concede, but what choice did she have? This—Jared—was what Susan and Brady wanted for their daughter. "It's...okay."

Or would be. Someday. Somehow.

"I'm sorry."

"It's not your fault." No matter how much Kate would have liked to blame him for this, she couldn't.

If only she knew what to do next. "I want to see Cassidy."

Jared nodded. "Let's sign whatever papers Don has prepared, then go to the hospital."

Chapter Four

The children's wing of the hospital was painted with bluebirds, colorful flowers, and rainbows, but the cheery decor did nothing to ease Jared's growing anxiety. He'd been trying to come to terms with a divorce he didn't want and now he was about to become a guardian. A father.

A dad.

He thought about Brady's letter.

You've always wanted kids.

Jared had wanted to be a dad. After he and Kate got married, she was enthusiastic about wanting kids, but they'd agreed to hold off to concentrate on their careers. Still, he'd imagined having a family, the perfect family to go with his fantasy of the perfect marriage—two children, a fancy double stroller, and a fully loaded minivan. But when Kate's company exploded onto the PR scene, she resisted starting a family. And then the Seattle opportunity arose. He thought the promotion and transfer was a way to have the family he desired. He thought moving without her would make her see how much he wanted the new job. He thought she would change her mind.

But it hadn't. Instead, he'd wound up with a job that left him living alone and destroyed his marriage.

Divorce.

Jared hated that word. Divorce meant failure. He hated failing or losing at anything. But there didn't seem to be anything he could do about it.

He was the first to admit they'd both made mistakes that contributed to the collapse of their marriage, but whereas Kate called the problems irreparable damage, Jared believed they could work through them. He missed Kate so much. If only she would get off the divorce kick and give their marriage a go...

Jared waited in the lobby for her. He would have preferred driving together, but she'd wanted a few minutes by herself. He didn't like her being alone when she was tired and stressed, but he understood. Their lives had been changed completely. Whatever the future held, however, they were in this together.

"Sorry." Kate's steps echoed on the tile floor. "I couldn't find a parking place."

Her red eyes suggested she'd been crying again.

He wished she would let him help her get through this. "I just arrived."

She adjusted the strap of her purse. "I hope Cassidy's okay."

"Don said she would be."

"I know, but there's okay and there's okay."

Her nervousness reminded him of the first time he invited her home to meet his family. She'd brought flowers and a bottle of wine. Kate had been pleasant, personable, perfect. He'd later discovered she'd bought a new outfit and had her hair done that day. Her efforts had touched him and taken their dating to a new level.

Jared took her hand in his. "Let's find out how okay Cassidy is."

As they followed the yellow bricks painted on the floor and stepped onto the elevator hand in hand, he felt as if nothing had changed between them and they were still together. Still in love.

Those had been the days.

He'd been attracted to Kate since the moment he first saw her, and that attraction had only grown once he realized her brain matched her beauty. They'd been a perfect match.

The perfect couple.

He missed their conversations, even their disagreements. He missed everything about her, from the sound of her laughter to the birthmark on her left shoulder. He especially missed the lovemaking. Their problems had never reached the bedroom. Yet, somehow the marriage had gone wrong.

Bad.

But that didn't mean it was over. Maybe he could make something new, something good, happen between them to show Kate they could still be together.

He stopped at the nurses' station. "I'm Jared Reed, and this is Kate Malone. We're here to see Cassidy Lukas."

"I'm Rachel." The nurse smiled. "Don Phillips said you were on the way."

"How is she?" Kate asked.

"Cassidy is recovering well. She's in Room 402." The nurse picked up a file. "I'll make a note to have the doctor speak with you."

"Thank you," Kate said.

The small room had a chair in one corner, a sofa bed under a bank of windows, and a strange-looking crib against the far wall. The four-month-old baby girl slept oblivious to them or the machines connected to her. Cuts—some that had been stitched—and bruises—a few purple, others yellow—covered her arms and face. A white bandage was wrapped around her head.

A wave of protectiveness washed over Jared. This baby was his and Kate's responsibility.

"She's so beautiful," Kate whispered with a hint of awe in her voice.

Seeing the compassion in her eyes as she stared at the baby triggered something deep within him. This— Kate, him, and a baby—had been his dream.

She sighed. "Cassidy looks so much like Susan."

He saw the resemblance, especially around the mouth and eyes. "But she's got Brady's chin. I hope that doesn't mean she's as stubborn as he was."

Kate smiled wanly. "Let's hope not."

A stuffed bear and a basket of flowers sat on a cart. He read the cards. The bear was from Don Phillips and his wife. The flowers from Brady's work.

Why wasn't the room full of flowers, balloons, and cards? Where were all the visitors? Jared didn't get it. "Why is Cassidy all alone?"

"What do you mean?" Kate asked.

When his sister Heather gave birth to her third child, his family camped out in the waiting room. "There isn't anyone here with Cassidy. How come?"

"We're all she has."

"But friends. Surely Brady and Susan had some friends—"

"Who have their own families and lives," Kate explained. "Not everyone has a family like yours, Jared. A lot of people end up in the hospital alone. Even babies."

His mind accepted the truth of her words, but his heart and his upbringing rejected it. "That's not right."

"She won't have to be alone again. We can take shifts."

Shifts meant they wouldn't be together. He'd been apart from Kate for so long, too long, and wanted to make the most of this time. He needed to show her they could save their marriage.

"Is something wrong?" she asked.

The sight of the baby hooked up to beeping machines gave Jared second thoughts. His needs came a poor second to hers. "You want to take the first shift? I need to meet with Don."

Kate hung her jacket on the back of the chair, tidy as always. "That's fine."

But it wasn't with Jared. He didn't want to leave them alone. His gaze returned to Cassidy.

"The baby will be fine, too." Kate's voice sounded strained.

He wasn't worried only about the baby. Kate was tired. Jared wondered if she'd eaten lunch. He would be away for at least a couple of hours. What if she or Cassidy needed something?

"Go." Kate motioned to the door. "The sooner you're named personal representative, the sooner we get guardianship."

"If you need anything—"

"I'll call."

Would she? Kate, ever capable, never had called in the past. But he wouldn't stop hoping. "Please do."

He wondered if she heard him, or if it mattered to her because she didn't look up. He headed to the door.

"Jared."

He turned.

"It's been a full day and"—she moistened her lips—"please be careful."

The concern in her voice brought a smile. Maybe she wasn't so indifferent to him after all. Maybe he stood a chance. "I'll be back, Kate. Just as soon as I can."

Chapter Five

An hour later, Kate struggled to keep her heavy eyelids open. A sleepless night and overloaded emotions had taken their toll on both her body and her brain, but she wouldn't give in to the exhaustion plaguing her.

Not in Cassidy's hospital room.

What if the baby woke up and Kate didn't hear her?

Sure, nurses entered with regularity, but she didn't want to let Susan down. Or Jared. All Kate needed was a second wind.

As she stretched her arms, she wiggled her fingers. Caffeine would help, but she didn't want to leave Cassidy alone.

The minutes ticked by.

Kate's head fell forward.

Dazed and disoriented, she straightened. The smell screamed hospital, and Kate recognized where she was, but that didn't stop her from taking in the cream-colored walls, the overhead lighting, a bed couch, and a crib surrounded by noisy machines.

Cassidy.

The baby lay sound asleep. So small. So fragile.

And Kate's responsibility.

She sat ramrod straight with the balls of her feet pressed against the wall. Comfortable, no. But napping while on duty wasn't allowed.

Despite her brave words and determination, the thought of doing something wrong, of being unable to care for Cassidy the correct way, terrified Kate. She didn't want Jared to find her asleep on the job. He held all the cards, or in this case, the baby. She wouldn't give him a reason to doubt her child-rearing abilities.

Kate stared at the crib across the room.

The machines lit and beeped, but Cassidy didn't move. She hadn't made a sound, either.

Unease prickled the hair at the back of Kate's neck.

Check her.

She imagined Susan's voice saying the words, and a heaviness weighed down on Kate. She'd lived with fear and uncertainty her entire childhood, and she'd moved beyond the two since becoming an adult.

She'd put the past behind her, set goals, and achieved them. But now Kate had been tossed into a whirlpool of doubt and confusion. She hated feeling that way again, and the million what-ifs running through her mind paralyzed her.

She remembered Susan telling her about checking the baby during the middle of the night to make sure Cassidy was breathing. Kate knew Susan's fears were irrational and told her to take advantage of the free time and sleep herself. Susan had smiled but said nothing. Now Kate understood the new mother's anxiety, and she didn't like it one bit.

She shifted in her chair, uncomfortable with this needy, uncertain self.

Where was Jared? Shouldn't he be back by now?

Kate glanced at the clock.

Only an hour had passed. With the paperwork to submit to the court, he wouldn't return anytime soon.

She blew out a puff of air.

Jared.

Even if they disagreed most of the time, his presence would comfort her—distract her, especially if he gave her a dimpled smile, the kind that spread to his eyes. It had been months since she saw one of those. Not that she'd seen him, either.

A light blinked.

Kate scanned the bank of machines. Surely if something were wrong, a monitor would sound an alarm and alert the nurse who would come running.

She took a slow, deep breath.

Was this how her life would be from now on? Worried something terrible would happen? Worried she would somehow fail Cassidy? Worried she would disappoint Susan in the worst possible way?

If only Jared...

Kate shuddered. She had to stop. Now.

She didn't need Jared. She'd survived the majority of her life without him. He'd proven he wouldn't stick around forever, that if she didn't do what Jared wanted, he would leave. The realization provided resolve and courage, both of which she needed.

She could handle this. On her own. The way she'd always done.

All Kate needed to do was check the baby.

She slipped off her shoes, walked softly to the crib, and peered down.

The rise and fall of Cassidy's chest brought a rush of relief. The peaceful expression on her cute face blanketed Kate with warmth.

How could something so small make her feel so good?

She fought the urge to caress the baby's smooth cheek. The last thing she wanted to do was wake the sleeping infant.

Kate stood by the crib. Watching the machines, with all those blinks and blips, would keep her busy until Jared returned. And then it would be his turn.

But she realized with unexpected clarity, her turn

wouldn't be over. Her life would never be the same. Even after the divorce, Cassidy would always link Kate to Jared.

The implications, both past and future, swirled through her mind. There would be no tidy goodbye. No tucking away the memories and forgetting about him. No moving on without Jared a part of her life. They would spend the next eighteen years making decisions about Cassidy, a child who would rely upon them for everything—nourishment, shelter, nurturing, advice, and love.

The reality of what their new responsibility entailed hit full force. Kate stood frozen, assailed by a multitude of doubt. She and Jared couldn't agree on what television show to watch or what they would eat for dinner on the weekends they were home together. How would they agree on what to do with Cassidy? Until she became an adult?

Kate staggered back.

What on earth had Susan been thinking? Brady, too?

Raising a child was nothing like babysitting Jared's nieces and nephews. Kate had no idea how to be a...mom.

She gulped.

Motherhood had been an ideal, never anything real or attainable, just something she'd forgotten about when she realized her days as a wife were numbered. She didn't have a clue about being a parent. The only thing she knew was what kind of mother she didn't want to be. Her mom and others had shown her that.

And what about Jared?

He had no experience being a dad. Sure, he liked kids, but that was different from having your own, especially with his travel schedule. And once they were divorced...

Kate leaned against a wall. Having them raise their daughter might be what their best friends wanted, but how in the world would she and Jared do this?

* * *

"How will you do this?" Not even a lousy phone connection masked the concern in Margery Reed's voice.

Jared wanted to reassure his mother, but no words came. Not when he was as uncertain about this situation as the rest of his family—two of whom he heard voicing their opinions in the background.

"Raising a child isn't easy under the best of circumstances," his mother continued.

She meant his marriage. Or rather, his soon-to-be lack of one. The divorce had not only caught him off guard, but also the entire Reed clan. His father had encouraged him to accept the promotion and move to Seattle with the belief Kate would follow him. His mom had warned Jared not to push Kate into a corner. Like his dad, he'd assumed their marriage was more important than her career. Jared had been wrong.

"Being a single parent will be hard on Kate," his mom added.

"Don't worry." Especially since he was the one who would end up with Cassidy, but he wasn't about to drop that bombshell on them yet. "We'll figure it out. Reeds always come out on top."

"You sound like your father and Grandpa."

"Then, I'm on the right track." A flashing sign caught Jared's attention. The Burger Barn. It was dinnertime. He doubted Kate had eaten. He pulled into the parking lot and stopped behind a red pickup truck in the drive-thru line. "Remember what Grandpa said? Second place is for everyone else."

His mother laughed. "You'll be saying the same thing to Cassidy before you know it."

An invisible weight pressed against Jared. He had a good job and made recommendations to clients who invested millions of dollars in companies based on his word, but that responsibility was different than the parental kind. "Yeah. I guess I will."

"Chin up. You'll be a great dad."

Brady had written the same thing in his letter. Jared would do his best.

"I can't wait to meet our newest granddaughter."

He imagined her bragging to her friends about the

latest addition to the family. If only it was under happier circumstances.

"Would you like us to come to Boise to help you?" his mom asked. "We can be there tomorrow. Tonight if you need us."

Yes. Please.

He would like nothing better than to dump this mess in his mother's experienced lap. But Jared swallowed the words. He was in this on his own. Or rather, he was in this with Kate.

Once his family swarmed in on them, he and Kate would lose any chance of making this parenting thing work together. He wouldn't be able to show his wife what she'd given up. What they were both missing. What they could still have if only she weren't so stubborn.

Okay, a reconciliation was nothing more than a pipe dream, but he wasn't ready to accept the failure of his marriage completely—lawyers and divorce settlement aside.

Kate had never been comfortable accepting his family's well-intentioned advice and assistance. She reminded him of a stray cat they'd found living in their garage when he was a kid. The cat wanted to be petted, but would hiss and arch if it received too much attention.

The Reeds rode into town like the cavalry with a cloud of dust in their wake. His parents acted from hearts full of love, but it was better to stand back and get out of the way to keep from being trampled. If his family came to Boise, they would take charge. Kate would be pushed aside. Him, too. For once, Jared would concede that point.

Cassidy was his and Kate's responsibility.

"Thanks, Mom, but let's see how we do on our own first."

"We?" His mom's voice rose an octave. "As in you and Kate?"

"The two of us were named guardians."

She inhaled sharply. "But the divorce—"

"Isn't final yet," he interrupted, not wanting his mom to say anything bad about Kate. "And Cassidy needs both of us."

"Do you think...?" His mother's words trailed off.

Silence filled the line. No doubt his mom was curling strands of her frosted hair around her finger. Something she always did when she wasn't sure whether or not to speak up.

"What?"

"It's none of my business." The words rushed out, which told him she very much thought she had a right to ask.

Might as well get this over with. "Go ahead and ask, Mom."

"With Cassidy in the picture, will Kate change her mind about the divorce?"

"I hope so," Jared admitted. "That would be the best thing for Cassidy."

"Would it be the best thing for you?"

"Yes." Jared didn't hesitate with his answer. He wanted to avoid divorce at all costs.

"We love Kate, but please be careful," his mother said. "We don't want to see you hurt again."

Neither did he, but being with Kate when things were different between them hurt now.

The red truck pulled forward. "I've got to go, Mom. I'll talk to you later."

"We'll be here. Love you."

"I love you." Jared disconnected the call.

He had no doubt his entire family would offer their advice and help. That was what the Reeds did.

You have your family to support you.

Brady had written that in his letter. Jared did have his family's support. And he might need it more than he ever had. He hoped Kate recognized what a blessing the Reeds would be with Cassidy.

But instead of hoping to get Kate back, he needed to do something about it. Jared was taking a chance by putting their marriage—himself—on the line, but he had no other choice. She might say no, and he would be worse off, but she might say yes, and that was worth the risks. Because if she agreed...

Jared smiled. He would get back his wife, and the family he'd dreamed about would be his.

Chapter Six

The smell of grease wafted in the sterile air of Cassidy's hospital room. Kate's stomach growled, and her mouth watered.

Exhaustion, hunger, and hallucinating about food weren't the best ways to wake up. A couple of crackers from a nurse would take care of two of those things.

"How is Cassidy?"

The sound of Jared's softly spoken question brought a smile to Kate's face. She turned, saw him standing there, and tingles shot through her. Okay, most likely seeing the bag of takeout and the drink holder with two large cups in his hands caused the tingling.

Whatever his faults, Jared made sure she ate.

"She's doing well," Kate said. "She was awake for a bit."

"Shouldn't we whisper so we don't wake her up?"

"The nurse said noise wouldn't bother her. If we're too quiet, the baby will need total silence to sleep. The nurse recommended keeping music on in the house once we get home."

Wherever home might be.

Kate hoped Portland, at least until the divorce was final. She didn't want to imagine what would happen after that.

"Makes sense." Jared placed the bag on a table. "I brought double cheeseburgers, mustard and pickles only on yours, fries, and onion rings."

Her empty stomach cheered. "My favorites."

A beat passed. "I remember."

So did Kate.

They would grab lunch at a local burger joint and head to the park for an impromptu picnic lunch on the rare occasion when they were in town on the same day, and it wasn't raining. She remembered eating and lounging on a blanket until the ringing of their cell phones told them it was time to return to work.

"Thanks." She offered him a smile. "I needed this."

Mere words, however, didn't seem enough. Kate might not need Jared to be here, but she was happy he was. She would have to do something nice for him.

"Thank you for staying with Cassidy." Jared handed her food and a drink.

Kate wanted to gobble down her dinner, but she wouldn't allow hunger to replace good manners. She would wait until Jared was ready.

He stood by the crib. "Eat."

"I can wait." Kate sipped her soda instead. She needed the jolt from the sugar and caffeine. Jared's watchful gaze, however, made her uncomfortable. "What?"

He glanced back to the crib. "Let's eat before the baby wakes up."

She wasn't about to disagree.

Jared pulled his dinner from the bag, unwrapped his cheeseburger, and took a bite. He wiped his mouth with a napkin. "I don't know about you, but I'm starving."

Kate picked up a fry. "This hits the spot. I owe you."

"It's on me."

She hadn't meant financially, but she understood his response. They'd kept their bank accounts separate after they married. Every month, they each deposited an equal amount into a joint household account to cover the mortgage payment and other household bills. The method worked well, especially with splitting their assets for the divorce settlement. "Thank you."

"You're welcome."

They ate in comfortable silence, a difference from the negative undercurrents they'd encountered before their separation. She'd hated walking on eggshells when they rarely saw each other because of his traveling to clients and her getting the company off the ground.

Kate finished her soda, wiped her hands, and tossed the trash in the can. She headed to the crib.

"The nurse said the doctor might release Cassidy in two days, three at the most." Kate's fingers itched to touch the slumbering baby if only to prove she was real. "Did you and Don finish going through the paperwork?"

"Completed and filed." Jared stood next to her. His gaze focused on Cassidy. "Don hopes the court will appoint me personal guardian tomorrow so we can start the guardianship proceedings."

"And then the real fun begins."

Jared reached toward the baby before placing his arm at his side. "I've been thinking about the guardianship issue."

"Me, too." Kate stared at ten tiny fingers. "It won't be easy. We know nothing about babies."

"You're right, and this will be difficult on Cassidy. She doesn't know what's happening or where her parents went, so we need to make sure she's the priority."

"I agree." Kate looked at him. "We need to consider Cassidy and the effect on her with every decision we make."

Suddenly, the situation didn't seem so

overwhelming to Kate. She wasn't alone. She and Jared were discussing matters logically, rationally, without disagreeing. A positive sign. She only hoped they continued to get along.

Jared's natural smile sent her heart beating faster. "Sounds like a good plan."

His agreeing bolstered her spirits and gave her the courage to ask what had been on her mind. "Once Cassidy is released from the hospital, can I please take her to Portland with me? At least until the divorce is final."

"Another good idea." His gaze traveled from the baby to Kate. "My family can watch Cassidy when you're at work. Unless you have a better idea?"

Child care. Kate hadn't considered that, but a nanny or daycare made little sense when the Reed clan lived in the same city. And Susan wanted Cassidy to be part of a large family.

"I hadn't," Kate admitted. "Will your family mind?"

He laughed. "They'll be fighting over the baby to see who watches her first."

She should have known it wouldn't be an issue. The Reeds had circling the family wagons down to a science.

Kate clutched the edge of the crib, careful not to move it. "That'll be good for both Cassidy and me."

And Susan. That was what she wanted for her daughter. She must be smiling up in Heaven.

Except, would Kate see the recrimination in Jared's family's eyes? Sure, they invited her to dinner and gatherings, but they weren't happy about the divorce. Some had been vocal about it, which was why she'd stopped seeing them.

"This will be a good arrangement while we figure things out for the long term." His eyes zeroed in on a display with numbers. "I'll come down and help on weekends."

Her pulse kicked up a notch. "That would be great."

"Yeah, great."

His gaze locked with hers. The temperature in the room increased by ten degrees. Kate needed another soda or a glass of water or a...kiss.

She stared at the baby, who hadn't stirred.

A kiss was the last thing she needed—wanted. Her reaction had to be because of the situation. The grief following the deaths of Susan and Brady. The emotion of being named Cassidy's guardians.

Kate wouldn't allow herself to think otherwise. He'd mentioned the long term, which raised a question. "What about after the divorce?"

"The best *thing* for Cassidy is parents who are married."

Kate stiffened. She forced herself to look away from Cassidy and at Jared. "That's what Susan and Brady would have preferred. But in our case, a traditional family is not possible."

A beat passed. "It is if we didn't get a divorce."

His words hung in the air.

Not divorce?

That was the craziest idea Kate had ever heard. She almost laughed, except he wasn't smiling. The serious gleam in his eyes told her he wasn't kidding. Okay, she appreciated him suggesting a noble gesture for the baby's sake, but one of them had to be realistic.

"What difference would not divorcing make?" Kate loosened and then tightened her hands on the crib. "We hardly saw each other when we lived in the same house. Now we live in different states. Marriage would never work."

"Don't you want Cassidy?"

That wasn't fair.

"You know I do." Kate wanted the baby so much the fierceness surprised her. Once again, she fought the urge to touch Cassidy. "But staying married under our current circumstances—"

"Let's change the circumstances."

Hope squeezed her chest. Would Jared move back to Portland?

Eager to hear his answer, she leaned toward him. "What do you suggest?"

"I just..." He appeared to be at a loss for words. "Maybe things could be different between us."

Not good enough.

Kate wouldn't allow Jared back into her life, into

her bed, into her heart only to watch him leave and hurt her again. She let go of the crib. Unless...

Thinking about the wedding rings locked away in a safe-deposit box at her bank knotted her muscles. The weight loss had provided an excuse to take them off. To be honest, she never imagined putting the band and diamond solitaire on again.

"Things would have to be very different." A plan to accomplish that formulated in her head. It might work or cause more problems. She gulped.

Jared eyed her warily. "What do you have in mind?"

Kate couldn't believe she was considering this, but she would do anything to keep Cassidy. She rubbed her thumb over her bare ring finger. "A marriage of convenience."

His brows furrowed. "A what?"

"A marriage in name only for Cassidy's sake."

A vein throbbed in Jared's neck. He glanced at the baby again. "You'd go for that kind of arrangement?"

She inhaled sharply because she had doubts, but she was desperate. Logically, that kind of marriage could work. Emotionally...

No, she wouldn't go there.

"I would." Kate touched the crib with her left hand. This was not only the best solution for everyone involved but also the best option to make sure Cassidy stayed with her. "How about you? Would you agree to a marriage of convenience?"

Chapter Seven

"Jared?"

All he had to say was yes to Kate, but a marriage of convenience hadn't been Jared's solution. He wanted things to return to how they were. Well, better. This suggestion of hers sounded more like a Hail Mary pass in the final seconds of the championship game than a viable plan.

She bit her lip, a nervous habit she'd had since they met. "What do you think?"

That she was out of her mind.

At least insanity would explain the "in name only" proposition. He would rather believe her crazy than accept her rejecting him all over again. He still wasn't over what had happened. Jared sometimes doubted he ever would be.

When Kate said she wouldn't move to Seattle with him, he'd been upset. When she told him she was filing for divorce, the news had devastated him. And now this...

His jaw clenched. He just didn't get her.

This morning, drawn together in grief, he'd felt closer to his wife than he had in months. But now he saw Kate didn't want the same thing he did. She didn't want to save their marriage the way he did.

The realization made his decision more critical. With differing expectations, her solution could turn into a disaster and drive them further apart. That was the last thing he wanted. Especially with Cassidy involved.

"How would this work?" he asked, struggling to keep his voice steady.

"One of us would keep Cassidy during the week. Most likely me since your family can take care of her during the day," she explained, expounding on her plan with enthusiasm. Kate was a great one for planning. "We can spend weekends together, so people won't think we're separated."

Being separated, like divorced, would give him custody per the conditions of the will.

Jared weighed the options. Okay, he could work with weekends as long as she wasn't serious about this "in name only" stuff.

"We can alternate between Portland and Seattle," she continued. As she stared at Cassidy, the tenderness of Kate's gaze reminded Jared of how she used to look at him, and something twisted inside him. "Drive up on Fridays, come back on Sundays."

Weekdays apart, weekends together.

That was more than she'd been willing to do before. Some of his unease disappeared.

Sure, a long-distance marriage wasn't what he wanted. Jared wanted Kate in Seattle full-time, but this was a step in the right direction. She would fall in love with the city the way he had, and with the attraction buzzing like static between them, physical chemistry would soon take over. Kate would realize they belonged together and move north.

Now that would be a very convenient marriage. And worth whatever challenges and commuting the next few weeks and months held if things worked out the way Jared hoped they would.

"So...you, me, and Cassidy will be together on the weekends," he stipulated.

"Well"—she wet her lips—"mostly together. We would share the same house. You and I would remain legally married. We just wouldn't do some things other married couples do."

Uh-oh, but the words "legally married" meant not divorced—key point.

"So you'd continue to keep your name," he said, making sure he understood the intricacies. "We'd keep our finances separate. We'd live apart except on weekends."

They'd lived that way before the separation. It had worked well for them.

Nodding, she scuffed the toe of her shoe against the floor. "It also means we won't be, um."

"What?"

"Romantic."

She was serious. He smiled, hoping to lighten her mood. "With a baby around, that's a given."

For now.

If they spent a weekend in Portland, his family could watch Cassidy, so he and Kate had time alone to rekindle their romance.

"It's not just romance," she clarified, her voice tight. "It's also, you know..."

Afraid he knew what she meant, Jared's stomach clenched. But he wanted her to spell out the rules in case he was wrong. "I don't know."

"Sex." The word came out fast and hard.

He figured as much. Still, he wanted her to state the rules. "What about it?"

"There won't be any."

There had been no sex for a while. Jared didn't like that, but he assumed once they were back together...maybe not right away, but eventually. He rocked back on his heels. "No sex for how long?"

She bit her lip again.

"Kate?" he pressed, wanting an answer.

"Never," she mumbled.

He stared at her in disbelief. "Ever?"

She blushed. "Correct."

No way. She couldn't be serious. Jared started to speak before stopping himself. He glanced at the baby. Seeing her serene face calmed him. "But we're married."

"Yes, but we'll stay married for Cassidy, not each other," Kate explained as if she were ordering a cup of coffee, not talking about their future together. "That's why it's called a marriage of convenience."

"That's totally inconvenient." The words came out harsher than he intended, but *come on*! What she suggested was…

Stupid.

No sane person would agree to that.

She shrugged, but she didn't appear indifferent. The way her fingers clutched the crib white-knuckled with one hand told him she wasn't joking around.

"Let me get this straight." Jared imagined living in the same house with Kate and not touching her. Impossible. "There would be no fooling around?"

"No."

"What about kissing?"

"I—I'm pretty sure kissing goes against the rules of an 'in name only' marriage.'"

Screw the rules.

That wasn't a marriage.

Sure, he was managing the celibacy imposed by their separation, but he didn't want to live like that forever. With his wife. "You think we can live like that?"

"If we have to." She leaned over the crib for a moment before letting go and touching his arm. "For Cassidy's sake."

No way. He wanted to do what was best for the baby, but Kate was too passionate to spend her life in a sexless marriage. Sure, she might think she could for Cassidy's sake and hold out a while, but Kate wanted him as much as he wanted her. He would bet money on it because she still had her hand on him.

And that, he realized, would work completely in his favor.

It also gave him an idea.

A way to rattle Kate's neat little world and bring her back where she belonged.

With him.

Correction—with him and Cassidy.

"I've got to be honest with you," he admitted. "I don't think I can live like that."

She lowered her hand, and her gaze returned to the baby. "It's a lot to ask to put aside all your own, um, needs, and focus on the baby's. But all parents have to do that to some extent."

I hope you and Kate have worked things out. You told me she's a keeper, so hold on to her.

Brady's letter rushed back. He wanted his daughter raised by a married couple. And Jared wanted his wife back. Kate was a keeper. He'd known that after their second date. He hadn't been looking for one when they'd met, but there she was nonetheless. The thought of being divorced bothered Jared more than a sexless marriage did, but if his idea worked, neither of those things would be a future concern.

"What about other people?" he asked.

Her wide-eyed gaze jerked to his. "What?"

Aha. That got her attention. He had to keep going. Maybe he wasn't being totally fair, but the end result—a solid marriage for the baby and for them— justified his methods. "What if we saw others, discreetly, of course, so long as our actions don't affect Cassidy?"

"I—I hadn't thought about that."

From her arched eyebrows, Kate didn't like the idea, either. Good. This was working as he intended.

"I don't mean right away," Jared added smoothly as if he'd given this a lot of thought, not come up with the game plan as he spoke. But he wouldn't push too hard or she would bail completely like she'd done filing for divorce. "We can discuss dating others in, say, six months. Once Cassidy is settled, and we're more comfortable with the arrangement. I mean, marriage in name only."

Kate's gaze narrowed. "So, you're considering this?"

Jared was. He must be out of his mind, too. But his plan seemed sound, so he would go for it. "Seeing other people?"

"No, the marriage of convenience."

Mentally, he counted backward from ten. "Yes."

Her eyes widened with surprise, but she said nothing.

He forced himself not to smile. Keeping the opponent guessing was the way to go if he wanted to win. And he wouldn't lose. All he'd wanted was forever with her. Still, he needed to be honest about one thing. "But the no-sex thing is a deal-breaker for me. I won't live that way. Not even for Cassidy."

Kate dragged her upper teeth over her lower lip. "Have you been seeing other people?"

Jackpot. Jared had her right where he wanted her—curious about his social life without her. "No. I didn't think that was a good idea until the divorce was final."

"Oh."

He glimpsed relief in her eyes. "What about you?"

"Me? No." Her cheeks reddened. "I mean, with work and everything, I never considered dating."

But she would now.

And that, too, would work entirely in his favor. Kate trusted him. With all his travel, she had to—spouses who didn't made themselves paranoid. But if they weren't really married and she knew he was discreetly dating, she would never assume she was the only woman he wanted in his bed.

Which she was. But that was a card he wasn't ready to show yet. "So what do you say?"

A beat passed. "O-kay."

He released the breath he'd been holding. "Okay?"

"The marriage will be a legal one, not an emotional one." Her words didn't give him the warm and fuzzies, but hey, it was better than a divorce. "I'm willing to consider, um, seeing other people once we have the situation under control."

"Good." Because the discussion would never come up. Soon, Jared would have Kate right where he wanted her. He would have what he wanted—his wife in Seattle with him, in his life, and in his bed. Someday they would share a good laugh over all of this. "This is what's best for Cassidy."

And, Jared realized, it was the only way for him and Kate to save their marriage.

Chapter Eight

Later that night, Kate stood on her hotel room's balcony. The crescent moon appeared painted on the star-filled black sky. A cool breeze ruffled her nightshirt, and she ignored the goose bumps on her arms and legs. She should be in bed, sleeping while she had the chance, but each time she closed her eyes, a million thoughts took over her mind.

What had she done?

The sound of the rushing water from the river below matched the turmoil raging inside her. She clutched the wrought-iron railing.

She'd never expected Jared to suggest they not divorce. Yes, he'd claimed he wanted to work things out, but those were just words. His actions for months had shown Kate he only wanted her in Seattle with him. That wasn't working things out. That was Jared winning his argument and getting his way.

Again.

But for now...

They wouldn't divorce. Except, they really wouldn't be married, either.

No sex.

She tucked her hair behind her ears. That would be...interesting.

Impossible.

No, not impossible.

If they kept their distance and locked their bedroom doors at night.

Correction, if *she* did that.

Jared appeared to have no problem agreeing to the rules so long as she didn't mind him seeing other people discreetly. Not that she had any interest in dating. But, like it or not, she understood his request. Sex had always been important to him. Obviously, his feelings for her had changed. That stung, but she had been the one to file for a divorce, and her feelings had changed, too.

Still, it wouldn't be easy.

They would need to set boundaries. The love between them may have died, but the physical chemistry remained strong—explosive as ever. Each time they touched, the pull of attraction drew them closer, which meant she would have to keep her distance.

Or find someone else.

The idea left her unsettled, sad even.

Kate took a deep breath.

This whole situation with Jared and Cassidy was so unbelievable. Kate glanced over her shoulder at the cell phone on the bed. She needed someone to talk to, only…

The one person she wanted to call, the one person she counted on to help her, could no longer answer the telephone.

Susan.

A wave of grief washed over Kate. She hunched from the jumble of emotions—sorrow, confusion, frustration—that followed. Tears welled in her eyes, but she wasn't about to cry again. Not even in solitude with the inky darkness of the late-night sky to hide her.

This was a time for strength. No matter how weak she might feel.

Cassidy.

Kate had to think about the baby and what Susan had wanted for her precious daughter:

She can have what we didn't have growing up. I need that for my child. Grandparents, aunts, uncles, a ton of cousins. Do you understand? I want you to understand this, Kate, and support it. I need you to be a part of Cassidy's life no matter what has happened with you and Jared.

And Kate understood, and she would be in that little girl's life.

To make Susan's dream for her daughter come true, Kate would do anything. That included spending the next eighteen years being married in name only to Jared Reed.

The cost and difficulties would be worth it to provide Cassidy with a mother and a father who loved her unconditionally. The pattern of Susan's and Kate's childhoods, full of uncertainty and instability and fear, would not repeat.

Whatever it took.

That was the bottom line for Kate.

She prided herself on her control and the ability to do what was necessary to achieve a result. Those skills would be as critical as ever now that Cassidy's wellbeing and future depended on Kate's action. She would push aside her emotions and live knowing Jared would be called her husband, but he would never really be hers again. By making practical, meaningful decisions for herself and Cassidy, Kate would give Susan what she asked of her best friend.

Kate would become the perfect mother.

Because that was all she could do.

* * *

At the hospital the next morning, Kate juggled a drink holder and a bag from Starbucks. The aroma of the freshly brewed house blend coffee made her crave a sip. After another restless night, caffeine would help her overcome her tiredness. But first, she wanted to see Jared.

No, Cassidy.

Kate was here for the baby.

She opened the door to the hospital room with her shoulder, took a step inside, and froze.

Both Jared and Cassidy were asleep. The tired part of Kate was envious, and her overwhelmed emotions found the scene heartwarming. Jared slept on the sofa bed with an arm outstretched toward Cassidy.

Kate's heart constricted at the sweet image.

Had he fallen asleep touching the baby?

At that moment, she could almost believe Cassidy would solve their marital problems and make them the perfect couple once again. But a few seconds of daydreaming was all Kate would allow herself because she knew better.

She swallowed a sigh.

Not even the precious baby would bridge the gap that pushed Kate and Jared apart. He hadn't wanted to wait to start a family. Kate's company, her employees, and her dreams hadn't mattered to him. He'd wanted her pregnant and in Seattle.

With him.

No compromise.

No discussion.

But when to have children had been only one issue.

Sure, he suggested marriage counseling, but only to visit a therapist who was a friend of his family and would take his side. The way his parents, siblings, aunts, uncles, and cousins had.

Misgivings over this marriage of convenience exploded.

Her heart beat triple time.

Their differences—what they wanted from their lives, their career, and pretty much everything—wouldn't just go away with a sweet baby to raise. Divorce or not.

Panic threatened to overwhelm her. Kate placed the bag and drinks on the bed table. She wanted out.

Now.

That would be the safest—the best—thing for her.

As she removed the food, she looked at Jared and Cassidy.

Her best friend's beautiful baby girl.

Unfortunately, there was no getting out of this.

Kate's heart rate slowed. She took a breath and another. No matter the turmoil inside, she had to remember who she was doing this for—Cassidy. Susan and Brady, too.

More in control, Kate pulled out the fresh fruit bowls, pastries, forks, and napkins.

Jared stirred on the sofa bed. As he stretched his arms over his head, his gaze zeroed in on Cassidy before looking at Kate. "You brought coffee and a continental breakfast buffet."

Ignoring his charming smile, she picked up a scone. "I figured you might be hungry."

"Thanks. I am."

Jared stood, his shirt wrinkled and his pants creased. He was sleep-rumpled and adorable, reminding her of when he'd come straight home after a long flight and tumbled into bed with her. Sleep had been the last thing on either of their minds. No matter how tired they'd been.

Heat emanated from deep within her.

He grabbed a pastry. "Is something wrong?"

No sex. No fooling around. No kissing. Seeing other people discreetly.

She tore a piece off her scone. "Why do you think anything's wrong?"

"Well, you lost your best friend, gained a child, and you have your tongue between your teeth, which is what you do when something's on your mind."

She didn't know what to make of his observation.

"There's a lot on my mind." But she wouldn't dare admit making love to him was one of them. "That's how it will be for a while."

"A long while, I'd imagine." He sipped his coffee. "This hits the spot. You went above and beyond as usual."

As usual.

Kate ate her scone, but having breakfast like this was weird. Their life together had been one way, they'd separated, and now they would reunite, but everything would be different. She wasn't sure how to act or what to do, but pushing the hair that had fallen across his forehead into place wouldn't be a good idea.

"Did you sleep?" Jared asked.

"Some." She guessed four hours after exhaustion had extinguished the thoughts in her head. "How about you?"

"I slept pretty well." He rubbed his neck. "Though the sofa bed was about as comfortable as a seat in coach on a trans-Pacific flight."

Kate glanced at Cassidy. "How did the baby do?"

"She fussed a bit." He walked over to the crib. "It took a while to get her to take a bottle."

"You fed her?"

"I did." His mouth quirked in a crooked smile. "I got to hold her, too."

No fair. Kate's skin prickled. "The nurse wouldn't let me do that."

Laughter glimmered in his eyes. "You must not have the right touch."

His lighthearted tone told her he was only kidding, but his words stabbed Kate's heart like a dozen daggers. She'd wanted to hold Cassidy and feed her, too, but the nurse had said no. Kate hadn't taken it personally. Until now.

"They disconnected the machines," he explained. "That's the reason I got to hold her."

Kate felt foolish. She had to stop with all the

insecurities plaguing her. "That means Cassidy is improving. And if she's released early..."

"I'm meeting with Don this morning to discuss the guardianship." Jared's tone brought reassurance. "Don't worry. This will work out. I promise you."

He'd promised to love her, in good times and in bad. That had lasted a little over two and a half years. Cassidy needed them together for the long haul.

A shadow of doubt crossed Kate's heart. "We have to make this work."

"We will."

She wanted to believe him, but leaving their problems—and the emotions associated with them—in the past wasn't easy. Not trying would be easiest, but what choice did she have?

None.

Not if she wanted to fulfill Susan's request.

And Kate did.

All they needed to do was be civil to each other on weekends. Anything more was asking for trouble.

She removed her jacket. "I guess you'll be off now."

He took a sip of coffee. "I don't mind staying a while."

But she did.

Yes, they would have to work together for Cassidy's sake, but Kate wanted space. The way he looked, the words he said, her body's response to him. She was too upset to think clearly. She would be better off alone with Cassidy so she could get used to how life would be once they got home.

"Don't you have to meet Don?" Kate asked.

"Yes, but I have time." Jared's gaze returned to the baby. "Cassidy needs her family with her."

Family.

Kate's head swam. She sat in the chair.

Her entire life, she'd dreamed of being part of a family. Sometimes she had been, until fate or the state of Oregon interfered. She was a member of the Reed clan by marriage. But now with Cassidy and Jared, the three of them would be their own family, too.

The baby screeched.

The sound, more pterodactyl than human, pierced the silence of the room. Kate jerked to her feet, and Jared hurried to the crib. He picked up the baby as if he'd been doing this all his life, not random nights when they babysat his nieces and nephews.

The crying continued.

He rocked Cassidy in his arms and then...quiet.

Kate stared in amazement.

"Good morning, Princess." Jared cuddled Cassidy close, and Kate's heart lurched. "Did you have sweet dreams?"

Her mouth went dry.

She'd never experienced the ticking clock with its overwhelming desire to have a baby. But seeing Jared with Cassidy in his arms sent Kate's world spinning off its axis. He'd always said he wanted children, but for the first time, she saw he was meant to be a dad. An incredibly sexy, desirable dad.

"Want a turn?" he asked.

She wanted...him.

No, Kate corrected. She wanted to hold the baby. "Please."

She cradled the warm, wiggly girl against her, supporting the baby's head and neck the way she'd read online last night. She'd known this from being Aunt Kate these past couple of years in the Reed family, but reminding herself of what was required wouldn't hurt.

Cassidy made a sucking motion with her mouth.

"She likes you," he said.

Kate's heart bumped. "She's hungry."

She touched her finger to the baby's tiny hand. Little fingers wrapped around hers.

An instinctive reaction? Kate didn't care. All she knew was she could get used to this.

And that scared her.

She'd lost everyone she'd loved. How would this be any different?

It probably wouldn't.

Her chest tightened. "You can take her."

Jared placed his hands on her shoulders. "It'll work out, Katie."

She wanted to believe him. Desperately.

Not divorcing him was the best thing for the baby, Kate knew that in her heart. But with his touch burning through her blouse fabric and his warm breath heating her blood, Kate wished she knew if this marriage was the best thing for her, too.

Because she wasn't sure.

She wasn't sure of anything.

Chapter Nine

As Jared sat behind the wheel of the idling rental car two days later, the reality of what he'd inherited slammed into him. He gripped the gearshift. Forget speeding around town in his fully restored 1966, cherry-condition Corvette. He needed a family car like the minivan he'd imagined, but that wasn't all.

He glanced at Kate in the passenger seat. Her whole package had come together nicely today with black pants, blue shirt, crystal jewelry, and shoes. The only thing missing—her wedding rings.

"Are you ready?" he asked.

Cassidy squealed before Kate answered.

With a glance in the rearview mirror, he checked the back seat. At least their VIP passenger appeared ready to leave the hospital. The little cutie.

Kate adjusted her seat belt. "Is the baby strapped in tightly enough?"

"Yes. Cassidy isn't going anywhere." The accident popped into Jared's mind. The baby was in the same model of car seat that had helped her survive the horrific crash. He'd known which to buy when he'd gone to the store yesterday. He would make sure nothing happened to her. "I stopped by the fire station, and they double-checked the car seat installation. The nurse also checked."

Kate glanced around the seat. "I wish we could see her face."

"The car seat has to face backward until she's at least two. We can buy a mirror to see her face tomorrow."

"I should ride back there with her until then."

"Is that what Susan did?"

"No, but if she had…"

Jared's heart hurt for Kate, but what-ifs would only make the grief process harder. With the work getting the estate in order, there had been little time to think about Susan and Brady. Once they were home, Jared and Kate needed to concentrate less on the to-do list and more on themselves and each other. "Do whatever makes you comfortable, Katie."

The baby made popping noises. At least Cassidy didn't seem to mind being in the car.

"Just drive," Kate said finally. "The baby seems happy."

That was good enough for him. He shifted the car into gear and released the brake.

Kate sucked in a breath.

"Nervous?" he asked.

"No. Why do you ask?"

The tightness around her mouth was a dead giveaway, but he wouldn't tell her. "We're on our own. No button to call the nurses' station if we need help. No one a few feet away to answer our questions. No one to pop into the room to give us a break."

"You sound nervous."

Jared shrugged. "Our lives have changed, but people deal with a new baby every day. We'll be fine."

"Yes, we will."

"Though I expected more than the nurse handing us the discharge papers, wishing us good luck, and sending us on our way." That had been surreal. "Most people have nine months to prepare for parenthood. You'd think they would give us a manual or instruction sheet."

She nodded. "Not much you can do with 'good luck.'"

That was more like the Kate he remembered and loved.

Come back to me, babe.

"At least we have Susan's baby books," Kate continued. "I've been going through them."

"Good." He turned onto the road. "One of us will know what we're doing."

"You seem to have a handle on parenting. Cassidy likes you."

"She has excellent taste." If only Kate felt the same way about him. Patience. He had to give them time to work things out. "But all I did was hold her."

"And walk her and rock her and sing to her," Kate said. "The nurses gave me a full report."

It wasn't right to take credit for doing what needed to be done. He might use the baby to get his wife back, but Cassidy's needs were the top priority. "It's the least I could do. The same as you."

"We have a steep learning curve ahead of us. Checkups, illnesses, diaper rash. I don't even want to imagine feeding her solids. What if she's as picky as Brady?"

We. Not I.

The plan would work. The knots in Jared's stomach loosened.

"Then we buy a side of beef and learn how to disguise vegetables as candy." He tapped his thumb against the steering wheel. Soon Cassidy would have a mommy and daddy who lived together and loved each other, too.

"What?" Kate asked.

He shot her a sideward glance. "You sound like a mom."

"Really?"

The hope in the one word surprised Jared. Kate always appeared so in control, so self-assured with everything, but her hopeful tone made her seem vulnerable and more...real. He liked that. "Yes, you sound like a mom."

A satisfied expression settled on her face. "That's the nicest thing you've ever said to me."

"I had no idea saying that works better than saying you look hot." He laughed. "I must remember that."

"Will that be your game plan when you need a night out with the boys?"

He smiled. "More like how to get out of the doghouse."

She smiled back. "Flowers and chocolate are good for that, too."

Yes. A point in his favor. Jared would pump his fist, but he was keeping both hands on the wheel.

A glance at the rearview mirror showed flashing lights rapidly approaching. A siren grew louder. Jared slowed the car and changed lanes. An ambulance roared past, its siren blaring.

The baby cried.

"She must not like sirens," he said.

"She might remember the sound and how she hurt after the accident."

He hadn't a clue what babies remembered. "That would make sense."

"It could explain how she doesn't like being woken up suddenly or with much noise." Kate reached back. "It's okay, Cassidy, we're right here."

The baby wailed.

Kate sighed. "I should have sat next to her."

"Maybe she'll settle down."

"I can climb back there."

The image of Brady's mangled car flashed through Jared's mind. He didn't want Kate to unbuckle her seat belt. "We only have a few miles to go."

The crying worsened. No matter what they said, nothing consoled Cassidy. Jared couldn't concentrate on the road. "Did you read anything in the baby books that would help calm her down?"

"No. She might be tired, hungry, wet. I have no idea." Kate twisted in her seat. "We'll be home soon, Cassidy. Do you miss your room? All your toys?"

The baby's cries squeezed Jared's heart. "I'm getting off the freeway at the next exit."

"We have to do something now."

"The radio," he offered.

"Noise might upset her more." Frustration laced each of Kate's words.

He understood. The wailing reverberated around him. "What do you suggest I do?"

When she didn't answer, Jared turned on the radio. A classical song played. Mozart, if he wasn't mistaken.

The baby screeched. So much for those songs for babies he'd downloaded.

Jared hit one of the radio's preset buttons. A

country music singer sang of lost loves and dented fenders. More crying. He pressed another button. A rock-and-roll tune filled the car with an electric guitar solo. Cassidy shrieked.

Tension ratcheted. Kate grimaced. "This isn't working."

The baby hiccupped between her sobs.

Jared wouldn't give up. He hit the AM dial and searched the stations, stopping when he heard stock quotes.

"Why are you putting on this station?" Kate reached for the radio. "It'll make her—"

Cassidy stopped crying as if someone had flicked an off switch.

"No way." Kate's arm hovered in front of the ON/OFF button before she placed her hand on her seat. "How did you know financial news would work?"

"Brady listened to this."

As a reporter spoke about an upcoming meeting to discuss interest rates, the baby squealed a happy noise this time.

"We'll have to add the money station in Portland to our presets," Kate said.

"It's one of mine."

"Then it might be one of mine. I rarely listen to the radio. I prefer to put on an audiobook."

He wasn't surprised. "Multitasker."

"I try to maximize my productivity. That will be more important now with Cassidy."

"You can do whatever you set your mind to." He wanted to reassure Kate. Who was he kidding? He wanted to take her in his arms and kiss some sense into her gorgeous head. "We'll both do whatever it takes."

"You sound so sure."

"I am."

"Aren't you worried about the future?" she asked.

"All we can do is our best."

"What if that's not enough?" She leaned her head against the seat. "All these things keep running through my mind."

"Like what?"

"I wonder what Cassidy will remember as she grows up. How long until she forgets Susan and Brady?"

"We'll keep their memory alive. We can tell her stories about Brady and Susan, so Cassidy will always remember and love them. And we'll take her to Maine to meet her grandparents."

"You've been thinking about this."

"Yes," he admitted. "It was hard not to when I was going through Brady and Susan's things. I realized that's one reason they chose us. Who better to keep their memory alive in their daughter's life than their best friends?"

Kate nodded.

He glimpsed affection in her eyes.

Unexpected emotion rushed through him, and

Jared struggled to maintain his composure. "I set aside some items for Cassidy, but there's probably stuff I haven't thought of keeping since guys aren't programmed that way."

"You're not like most guys, Jared Reed." Kate touched his arm. "Most guys wouldn't have done half of what you did this week. And fewer would have considered what to save for a four-month-old baby."

As she pulled her hand away, Jared wished she would keep it there. Still, her words gave him hope that one day soon they would put the past behind them and be a real family. The way Susan and Brady had wanted. The way Jared wanted. He only had to persuade Kate to want them to be a real family, too.

Chapter Ten

In the nursery, Kate taped the lid of the box containing toys and board books. She glanced at Cassidy.

Secure in her stroller, the baby patted the activity bar with chubby fingers.

The sight brought much-needed comfort. After two days of sorting through items at Susan's house, a heavy sorrow had taken permanent residence in Kate's heart. She made a conscious effort to breathe.

"All done," she announced to Jared.

"Good timing," he said, looking as attractive in shorts and a T-shirt as he did in a suit and tie. "We have to leave for the airport in a few minutes. Though with this weather, the flight might be delayed."

Thunder and lightning had set an ominous mood.

Sheets of rain fell from the dark, gray skies. The constant pelting against the roof had worsened with each passing hour. The dreary gray fit Kate's mood better than the warm, sunny days they'd had all week. Finally, the heavens were mourning the loss of Susan and Brady, too.

Except Cassidy's cheery disposition suggested nothing was wrong. She played with the spinning toy in front of her with glee. And why not? She was home, in the bedroom her parents had spent months decorating, lovingly painting pink and yellow stripes and stenciling flowers and butterflies. Cassidy might not notice the details, but the baby must sense she was where she belonged.

Unfortunately, she wouldn't be here much longer.

On Monday, the house would be put up for sale.

Poor Cassidy.

She had no idea what was in store for her. A part of Kate didn't want to leave Boise and take Cassidy away from the place Brady and Susan had called home.

"Hey." Jared tapped Kate's shoulder. "You okay?"

Not trusting her voice, she nodded.

"It'll be hard." His words matched her thoughts. "But we have to."

Kate nodded again. Selling the house made sense but left her with a severe case of guilt for taking the baby to Portland.

He carried the last box from the nursery and added it to the pile of stuff in the living room. Movers would transport everything to her home in Portland. The rest of the items would be sold or donated to charity.

Getting rid of a houseful of possessions seemed sad and wrong. She wished Susan and Brady were alive, and none of this had ever happened. If only...

Kate crossed her arms.

As the rain stopped, sunlight streamed into the room through the nursery's windows. The rays, defined by the particles in the air, surrounded the stroller. With a peal of giggles, Cassidy reached toward the sunshine.

The baby, who had never seemed so animated before, mesmerized Kate.

"What does she see?" Jared asked from the doorway.

"I don't know," Kate admitted. "Maybe she can feel the sun's warmth. Susan called it a sun kiss."

Kate wanted to reach out and grab hold of a ray, one of the sun kisses, to take to Portland. Her house needed a dose of sunshine badly. So did she. Perhaps Cassidy would bring some with her.

"Whatever the baby sees, she likes it." Jared sounded pleased.

Cassidy's little arms wiggled in the air as if she wanted to be picked up, but she wasn't looking at Kate or Jared. She wasn't crying, either.

"She's happy," Kate agreed. "That's what matters."

"The only thing that matters."

She took comfort in their ability to agree about the baby. The willingness to get along for Cassidy's sake would make things—okay, their future—easier.

"You've got a smudge of something on your cheek." Jared wiped her face with his thumb. "There. All gone."

His nearness disturbed her. He smelled good—a mix of fresh soap and raw earth from his work in the yard. "Th-thanks."

His gaze captured hers. "You're welcome."

Kate expected him to lower his hand. He didn't.

She waited.

Common sense told her to look away, but she didn't want to listen. Cassidy cooed and giggled, so there was no need to check on her.

"It's weird not going with you," Jared said.

"You have important business to finish up here."

"I know, but..."

His serious tone worried her. "What?"

He didn't answer.

She searched his face for a sign as to what he was thinking but found nothing. "Jared?"

"It'll be strange not having you"—he looked at the baby—"and Cassidy with me."

Cassidy.

This was about the baby.

Kate ignored the twinge of disappointment inching along her spine. She should be happy he cared so much about Cassidy already, so he wouldn't walk away again.

What was she thinking?

Jared might have left her the way everyone else had because she wasn't important enough for him to stay, but he would never desert the baby. "You'll see her next weekend."

"And you."

What he said shouldn't have affected Kate, but an unexpected lump formed in her throat. Jared had been a rock, supporting her during the emotional funeral service and boxing up Susan and Brady's house. He'd kept things moving and Kate going. Suddenly a week apart seemed like forever.

"Kate..."

The way he spoke her name made her pulse quicken.

"I'm happy we had time together this week," he said.

Her temperature shot up.

His lips curved in a half smile. "I'll miss you."

Her mouth went dry.

Jared lowered his face toward hers.

He was going to kiss her.

Her heart slammed against her ribs.

Grief, loss, exhaustion. Those emotions explained the physical reactions she was having to him. That was all her body's responses were, all they could be.

She should step back, put distance between them, but Kate didn't want to move away.

"It's time we headed to the airport," he whispered and kissed her forehead.

At the brush of his lips, relief mingled with regret.

A silly reaction. A good thing she and Cassidy were leaving.

Kate appreciated all Jared had done this week. She'd leaned on him, more than she ever had in the past, but she had to get used to being on her own again. A peck on the forehead, a tender glance, and a sincere word changed nothing. She was the one who had to juggle her routine with the baby's schedule.

Sure, Kate had misgivings, but she could do it. She'd always done everything herself.

But the thought didn't cheer her up. After this week with Jared, it only made her feel a whole lot worse.

* * *

Back in Portland, the telephone rang. With a grimace, Kate left the pile of pink- and pastel-colored laundry on the couch and ran to the kitchen. She should have turned off the ringer because the noise might wake Cassidy.

"Hello." Kate sounded rushed and frustrated. She didn't care. People she knew called her cell phone.

Only strangers dialing wrong numbers and telemarketers used the landline. She only kept it because of her cable company's discount for bundling TV, Internet, and telephone services.

"Hello, Kate."

The sound of Jared's voice brought a rush of anxiety. He never called on the home number. "Is something wrong?"

"No, I wanted to see how you and Cassidy are doing."

"We're, um, okay." Kate tried to muster enthusiasm, but she was an absolute failure at motherhood. Talk about on-the-job training at its worst, and she only had the baby in the morning and after work. The tremendous rush of relief and guilt each time she dropped off Cassidy at Jared's parents' house or picked her up at one of his sisters' houses was killing Kate, but she couldn't imagine being the full-time caretaker. Of course, the weekend was coming up. "We're adjusting."

Sort of.

"That's great." He sounded pleased.

"Yes, great." So long as she continually held Cassidy, only slept a few hours a night, and let the house go. Kate held the receiver with her shoulder and folded a pink onesie. The amount of laundry one baby generated amazed her.

"My mom says Cassidy's grown."

Kate attributed the baby's weight gain on her own

exhaustion. How much could a baby grow in less than a week? "She's still the same diaper size."

"My sister uses cloth diapers. Do you want to use them?"

"No." The word tumbled from Kate's mouth. She struggled to keep up with the laundry now. "Brady and Susan used disposables. Let's not change more in Cassidy's life."

Or mine.

"That's an excellent point."

Thank goodness, he agreed. Kate folded a burp cloth and made a mental note to buy more of them to protect her clothes.

"Do you need anything?" Jared asked.

You.

Strike that.

She needed an extra six hours a day to catch up with work at home and at the office. Despite the books and magazine articles she'd read, combining a career with motherhood required a tricky balance. One she wasn't close to mastering.

"No, thanks. I'm figuring things out." Or would. Getting used to having another person completely reliant upon her wasn't easy. She had no idea how other moms managed, especially those without a partner to help. "Though I see the benefit of maternity leave now."

Kate had dreamed of a smooth transition, of how wonderful being a mother and working a fulfilling job would be. Reality crushed her expectations. Her life at home was a far cry from the perfect baby who slept at night and smiled all day long. At work, she finally understood the undercurrent of tension between the women in the office who had children and those who didn't.

Exhausted and entirely unorganized, she was lost figuring how to make things work when all she wanted was a nap. Kate folded a lavender sleeper.

"Would taking time off help?" Jared asked.

Oh, no. What should she say? "It, um, might."

"Is a leave of absence a possibility?"

"No. Not right now." A part of her felt guilty for not spending this week with Cassidy, but she wouldn't admit that to Jared. Since she owned the company, she wouldn't have to qualify for family leave. She could stay home, but that might negatively affect her clients and employees. "What about you? Can't you take paternity leave?"

"Me?" His voice cracked.

"Your company must offer family leave."

"I…" Silence filled the line. "I hadn't considered that."

Of course he hadn't. "It should be in your company's benefit policies, or ask HR."

He said nothing. "I'm not sure my boss would go for that, but I'll look into it."

Yeah, right. Jared's lack of enthusiasm for the idea told her one thing. "I shouldn't have brought it up."

"You sound tired."

She was. Only sleeping in three- to four-hour bursts drove a person to exhaustion. Ever since arriving in Portland, Cassidy wouldn't sleep during the middle of the night. The baby wanted to be held, rocked, walked, or a combination of the three. So Kate did that, and she was feeling the effects. She'd fallen asleep at lunch today. "It's been a busy week."

"I know how that goes."

Jared might think so, but he didn't. He couldn't.

Once upon a time, before pink clothing, bottles of formula, and wet diapers had become a way of life, Kate believed she'd known the definition of a busy week.

She hadn't even been close.

Not until Cassidy.

But Kate couldn't tell him that or he would think she was unable to cope. She needed him to believe she was a good mother, so he would stay onboard with their arrangement and allow her to keep Cassidy. This tiny baby was the closest and the last remaining member of the only family she'd ever had. She wouldn't lose her.

Not like Kate had lost Jared.

"Where are you?" she asked.

"Raleigh, North Carolina."

"Weren't you going to Chicago?"

"Change of plans. I'm flying to Portland on Friday, and I'll take the train to Seattle on Sunday night."

Kate glanced around the house. The boxes from Boise remained unpacked. The clutter and mess embarrassed her. She wanted the house to be perfect when Jared arrived. "Do you need a ride from the airport?"

"I'll use a ride service."

"I don't mind."

"Don't worry about me."

"But I do." The words escaped quickly. "I mean, not all the time. But sometimes."

She should shut up before she made a bigger fool of herself. Maybe she needed another nap. Or a good night's sleep.

"I worry about you sometimes, too. So that makes us even."

The scales would never be equal, but she appreciated the sentiment.

"I'd better get going. I have work to finish. I'll call you later."

"Only if you have time." She had stuff to do, too. Her list of things to check off by Friday kept growing by the minute.

"I'll make the time."

"For Cassidy."

"And you. I miss both of my girls."

"Your girls miss you." Kate had missed him, more than she imagined she would.

His rich laughter filled the phone. "Kiss Cassidy for me. And here's one for you."

Smack.

With that, he hung up.

A burst of heat pulsed through Kate's veins. Too bad a real-honest-to-goodness-husband-to-wife-kiss from him wasn't an option because she wanted one.

Stop.

She shouldn't have those kinds of feelings about Jared.

She'd told him not to kiss her. She'd told him they would discuss seeing other people in six months. She'd told him their marriage would not be emotional.

But now, those were the things she wanted from him.

Chapter Eleven

The porch light wasn't on, and the door was locked. Since Kate had filed for divorce, Jared no longer had a key to the house he still owned with her. With a frown, he stabbed the doorbell once.

A minute ticked by.

And another.

Not good.

He hadn't known what to expect when he arrived, but his hope that she would be happy to see him plummeted.

As he stood outside in the dark, he feared she'd changed her mind about their arrangement. He jammed his finger against the doorbell again.

After one more minute passed, Jared pulled out his cell phone, but the door opened.

She held a flushed, crying Cassidy. "Sorry I took so long."

Frustration filled Kate's voice. He wanted to wrap his arms around her, but no matter how much he might want to embrace her, he couldn't. Not yet. They were tiptoeing across a tightrope with no net below. One wrong move and they would go splat. If that happened, their marriage was over.

He tucked his phone into his pocket. "Looks like you have your hands full."

No kidding.

The stark-white bandage around Cassidy's little head, the tears streaming down her round cheeks, and the "save me" gleam in Kate's eyes reminded him he wasn't the only one adjusting to a new set of circumstances. He wanted to help make things better for all of them.

She shrugged. "I was upstairs rocking her, but that only irritated her more."

"Are you having a tough time?" Jared ran his finger along Cassidy's smooth cheek.

The baby screamed.

He jerked his hand away. "Is she okay?"

"Yes." Kate rocked back and forth, and Cassidy stuffed her fist in her mouth and sulked. "She hates going to bed."

Jared didn't understand. His sister said babies slept a lot. "She might be hungry."

"She had a bottle."

"Gas," he offered.

"I burped her."

"Wet?"

"I changed her."

"Does her head hurt?" His brain did, from the noise and hunger. If he were a baby, he'd probably cry, too.

Kate glared at him. "Are you suggesting I don't know enough to take care of her?"

His hands, palms facing her, flew up in front of him. "No. You're doing great with Cassidy."

"I'm trying." Kate's shoulders slumped. "But she wants me to hold her. All the time."

That explained the dark circles under her eyes and why she had stains on her purple blouse and spots on her brown pants. Jared had never seen her with her hair haphazardly piled on top of her head and clipped that way. Even with a crying baby in her arms, how much she'd let her "whole package" slip surprised him.

Kate looking so...untidy...was weird. He didn't know what to make of it, but the tousled style was cute on her.

He appreciated she hadn't forgotten the most crucial piece of jewelry in her wardrobe. She wore her wedding set—a plain band and an engagement ring. The diamond sparkled as if newly cleaned. He wondered if she'd had it resized or was eating better.

Jared placed his luggage inside. Ready to be the

go-to guy, he closed the front door. Now facing his two girls, he wasn't sure where to begin.

Kate appeared to need a shoulder to cry on—or to sleep against. Cassidy, all teary-eyed and slobbery, clung to her.

He removed his jacket because of all the crying action going on. "I, uh, don't mind holding her."

The baby wailed.

Jared gritted his teeth.

Kate turned her away from him. "I've got her."

Barely.

He didn't know if he could do any better, but he owed it to both of them to try. "You do, but I'm here. Get some sleep."

"I'm fine."

But the tiredness in her eyes and the strain on her face showed she wasn't. The screaming baby was a big clue, too.

Kate, however, was being Kate and doing everything herself. He didn't want her handling child-rearing the same way she handled everything else in her life.

On her own.

"We're in this together." That much was true. Not that he knew what he would do once he had Cassidy.

Truthfully, holding a fussy—okay, crying—baby appealed to him as much as an IRS visit to discuss a tax return. Still, he had to help.

Kate gave no response. She swayed with the baby in her arms.

Tension simmered in the air.

Cassidy fussed and flailed.

Usually, when Kate—needing to do things her way—acted like this, they went head-to-head before having hot makeup sex. Jared wouldn't mind the latter, but that wasn't happening given their marriage-of-convenience rules. Besides, she didn't seem up for a disagreement, let alone a fight. The only thing she seemed ready for was bedtime.

He kind of liked it.

This new disheveled Kate was growing on him.

She appeared less in control, more vulnerable, and to be honest, sexier than her normally put-together, perfect, entire-package self. Not that Jared would admit that to her.

This haggard new-mom Kate needed him in a way the old PR-pro Kate didn't. That gave him hope for their marriage and raising Cassidy together. He couldn't wait to put an end to the in-name-only boundaries so they could be husband and wife and mom and dad in every sense of the words.

The baby punched the air like a fighter warming up for the second round.

"Please." Jared extended his arms. "I want to hold her. I missed her."

And you.

But he wouldn't go there.

Not yet.

Patience. He needed to tattoo the word on his brain, so he didn't push Kate too hard and too fast.

"Are you sure?" she asked, sounding uncertain.

"Positive."

With only the slightest hesitation, Kate handed him the baby. As her hand brushed his during the transfer, a shock stunned him.

Electric static? Physical attraction?

Or a little of both?

Jared didn't care which. Her soft skin against his, even if it had been for less than a nanosecond, reaffirmed they would overcome their marriage trouble.

"Hello, sweet pea," he said to Cassidy.

A sob greeted him.

"Now is that any way to say hello to me?"

Another cry.

As Jared cuddled the warm bundle, the baby's scent surrounded him. Not all sugar and spice tonight. He missed the fragrance of Kate's grapefruit shampoo. Cassidy smelled different...funny.

Formula? Or her diaper needed changing again?

She wiggled. Sighed. And then her entire body seemed to go boneless.

Magic.

Relaxed didn't begin to describe her content expression. Something inside of him melted.

Jared smiled. "Have you been giving Kate a hard time?"

Kate pushed an errant strand of hair into her clip. "Except for not sleeping, she's been great."

Cassidy reached with her chubby little hands to touch his chin but missed. "Ah-goo."

"Ah-goo?" Flattered, disarmed, he touched her nose. "Really?"

The baby grinned, all toothless gums and drool, and Jared was a goner. Okay, Kate might have had another reason for wanting to keep hold of Cassidy instead of control issues—baby love. "You're so cute."

Kate tsked. "You better be careful, or she'll have you wrapped around her little finger."

Too late.

"Nothing wrong with that." As he rocked, Jared glanced into the living room. The house, as usual, reminded him of a model home with every item in its place. Even the magazines on the coffee table were aligned perfectly. Not that he expected any less. Kate was a neat freak, plus a housecleaner came every other week. Except, something—boxes to be exact—appeared to be missing. "Did the movers come?"

She nodded.

"Where is everything?" he asked.

"Some items are in Cassidy's room. The rest is in the attic or garage."

"That must have been a lot of work."

Kate shrugged. "I hired someone to unpack and move the boxes."

As she always did whenever something needed to be done. She ran an efficient household for a person who worked sixty-plus hours a week.

Cassidy clicked her tongue. Her eyes widened, and she made the same clicking sound again. And again. And again.

His gaze returned to the living room. Same couch and coffee table, but the walls. "You painted."

"Last month, I updated a few things."

Tension crept into his shoulders. Update her life, update her house. Jared tried not to take the change personally. They were talking about a new paint color, not a new man. "The blue is nice."

Kate raised her chin. "I thought so."

At the challenge in her tone, he studied the living room.

The paint wasn't the only difference. Their wedding portrait no longer graced its spot of honor. New pictures, framed and matted botanical prints in black frames, however, hung on the wall. A straw-looking mat replaced the multicolored patterned rug they'd picked out one rainy afternoon at Pottery Barn. The bookshelves were emptier. Were his books missing?

"What do you think?" she asked.

"A lot of changes." Kate taking their home and making it hers made his stomach churn. He didn't like that. Yes, they'd been planning to divorce, but she could have waited until the dissolution was final.

Unless she'd divorced him in her heart, and the paperwork was a formality.

Jared shrugged off the idea. He couldn't believe that was true, not when he remembered what they'd had together. A few disagreements—okay, arguments—and differences of opinion shouldn't erase all the good times during the past four years. He would woo Kate back and win her heart.

But he had to ask. "Where's our wedding picture?"

"The frame is being changed to match the blue better."

Okay, good. She was fitting their married life into her new décor, not throwing the old away altogether.

The baby yawned.

He shifted her in his arms. "Are you tired, Cassidy?"

"Baaaah." The baby stuck her fingers in her mouth.

"Don't be fooled," Kate said. "She's only lulling you into complacency."

"She's a baby."

"She's a smart baby who won't sleep."

Jared laughed. "Tonight will be the night."

He hoped.

Kate rolled her eyes. "In your dreams."

His dreams revolved around his wife, not Cassidy. He'd missed making Kate smile. "Wait and see."

"I will."

The baby's eyelids fluttered shut before springing open. Kate crossed her arms. "Told you so."

"Patience." He rocked Cassidy and kissed her head above the bandage meant to keep the baby from pulling out her stitches and irritating the wounds still healing. "Isn't that right, sleepyhead?"

Kate arched an eyebrow. "You're not giving up?"

"Never. It's called perseverance." And the reason things would be back to normal between them soon.

"Or stubbornness."

"As long as I win"—he stared at the sleeping baby in his arms—"and I just did. It worked."

She inhaled sharply. "No."

"See for yourself," he whispered.

"You've got the touch, that's for sure," Kate said, and he hoped he'd get to use that touch on her. "Now, can you make the transfer to her crib without waking her up?"

He didn't know, but with Kate smiling at him, teasing him, reminding him of what they'd once shared, he would try.

Jared winked. "Watch the master."

"Where do I buy a ticket?"

The amused gleam in her eyes lit a spark in Jared. Maybe once he put the baby to bed, Kate would let him tuck her in, too.

Chapter Twelve

From the doorway of Cassidy's room, Kate watched Jared in action. He'd ditched his suit jacket downstairs, but that didn't matter. In his light blue dress shirt and striped tie, he looked more like a Hugo Boss model than a new father. Yet, his daddy instincts were on point.

That was incredibly attractive and a tad bothersome. A tiny part—one Kate hated to admit—resented him for succeeding where she'd failed.

As Jared gently placed Cassidy in the crib, Kate held her breath. When she let go was when the baby always woke up. This time, the baby remained asleep.

Kate stared in disbelief. She didn't get his success. Sure, Jared had babysat his nieces and nephews, but he'd done nothing like this. Still, he acted as if he'd tucked in Cassidy a million times—been a dad for years, not days.

He quietly backed out of the room. "Mission accomplished."

An angel must be on his shoulder, or he made a pact with the devil. Though she had to admit, he never lost when he set his mind to something.

Even with their divorce.

Kate bit her lip. He was getting his way as usual.

And that…burned.

For a second, she wanted to kick the door or make a loud noise, but common sense remained in control.

Or self-preservation.

Her fatigued body and brain needed a block of uninterrupted sleep. With some rest, she could finally be the mother she dreamed of being.

"If I didn't know better," Kate whispered, "I'd assume the two of you are in cahoots."

His face pinched. "It's been that bad?"

She didn't want to admit the problems she'd had this week. "Bad might be extreme."

"Let's go downstairs and talk, so we don't wake Cassidy." He kept his voice low. "I haven't been home in a while."

Kate remembered the last time he'd returned from a business trip on a Friday night. She'd helped him undress, not caring whether or not his shirt buttons stayed attached. They'd tumbled into the bed and knocked over the nightstand. And then they'd...

She took a deep breath.

As handsome as Jared looked tonight, she'd better put those memories behind her once and for all. Pretending to be in love when they hardly saw each other had been easy. Each weekend was like a honeymoon—apart for five days, together for two, repeat. And even though they would be doing the same thing now, she didn't want to fall into the same trap of believing what they had was real again.

It wasn't.

Or Jared would have never left Portland and her.

In the kitchen, Kate removed a brown paper bag from the refrigerator. "If you're hungry, I bought you a sandwich from the deli."

He took it with a chuckle. "Thanks."

"What's so funny?"

"I didn't expect dinner tonight."

She wasn't sure how to take that. "What were you hoping for?"

"A cup of coffee and a smile."

Thank goodness he wanted nothing else. "You hit the jackpot, then. You got a sandwich, the smile, and I brewed a pot of decaf. I bought beer, too, if you want one."

"After that crying, a shot of whiskey might be best." He sat on a stool at the breakfast bar and unwrapped his turkey and provolone sandwich. "But a cup of decaf will be great. Thanks."

"You're welcome."

See. They could be pleasant and platonic. No problem. This arrangement might work. Of course, once he started seeing other people...

No, she wouldn't go there now.

Jared loosened his tie. "Would asking for dessert be pushing it?"

Kate removed two mugs from the cupboard. The cups, white with mini blue coffee mugs painted all over them, had been a wedding gift from his coworker. She'd boxed them up, trying to put away the reminders of their marriage, but this week Kate unpacked them. Removing everything he remembered might upset him. "It depends on what you want and whether I have any to give you."

He rolled up his sleeves, giving her an enticing view of his forearms. "I want..."

Uh-oh. The desire in his eyes made her feel like she was the only treat he wanted.

He smiled, complete with dimples.

Her heart hammered against her chest.

Oh, boy. His smile was better than she remembered. All of him was.

Kate focused on the stove's clock, but she could tell his gaze was on her. She was in so much trouble.

"Cookies," he said finally.

"Cookies," she repeated, trying to regain control of her speeding pulse. "I have Oreos in the pantry."

"Another favorite of mine."

She didn't want him to think she'd gone out of her way. Sure, she'd purchased a few things he liked, but that was common courtesy. Nothing more.

Kate poured coffee into the two cups. "Well, I knew you were coming."

"You're the perfect hostess."

That was her intention. "Here you go."

As she handed him a steaming mug, her arm brushed his hand. Accidental, but heat burst at the spot of contact.

Distance.

She needed to get away from him, so she went to the pantry, pulled out a bottle of vanilla-flavored syrup, and the bag of cookies.

"Thank you," he said.

She wouldn't meet his eyes.

"Something wrong, Kate?"

You.

No, that wasn't correct. Her feelings were the problem.

Not only was she struggling with her grief over Susan and Brady's deaths, but Kate also missed Jared, even though she didn't want to. He'd left her before. In two days, he would again. Sure, they had a baby sleeping upstairs. But things between them hadn't changed. "Nothing's wrong."

Jared took a sip. "Perfect."

He liked his coffee strong and black. No cream or flavored syrups.

114

She added a shot of vanilla into her cup. "Someday, you'll join the rest of us and drink lattes and mochas."

"Never."

He was probably right. Jared and his entire family stuck to traditions. Big ones, like naming children after older relatives, and small ones, like how they preferred their coffee. She, on the other hand, had zero family traditions, unless eating Thai food while watching the Academy Awards every year counted.

Kate remembered acting out a love scene with Jared. The memory melted her insides like butter.

So not good. Shivering, she wrapped her hands around her mug.

"Are you cold?" he asked.

She was quite warm. Okay, hot. "I'm fine."

"Have you talked to the pediatrician about this not-sleeping-hold-me-all-the-time problem?"

She appreciated him changing the subject. If they discussed the baby, she could stop thinking of him as a, well, a man. One who she wanted to touch her again. "I'm not sure I'd call it a problem, but no, I haven't."

"What about my parents?" He picked up his sandwich. "Does she act the same way at their house?"

"Cassidy has no issue napping there during the day, but when she's here at night, sleep becomes a foreign word."

"Her internal clock might be screwed up."

"Susan would have mentioned that. I remember when she told me the baby had slept four hours during the night. She'd sounded like a new woman."

"Cassidy might have gotten spoiled. At the hospital, she had round-the-clock care and attention."

"The books say you can't spoil a baby." Besides, Kate couldn't spoil her if she wanted. Not working all day. "Why so many questions?"

His interest confused her. Jared, like the other male Reeds, might hold the babies during family get-togethers, but they never joined in the baby talk. Even though his father was only in his sixties, the man was a throwback to the 1950s view of traditional marriage and encouraged his sons to follow suit. Jared straddled the line, which was better than wanting her to wear an apron, lay out his slippers and tablet, and have a cocktail and dinner for him when he walked in the door. One year for Christmas, his kids had pitched in and bought him a retro smoking jacket as a joke. The gift had been a huge hit.

"I need to know what's going on," Jared said.

His taking the new responsibility pleased Kate. Perhaps, he wouldn't follow his dad's lead, but she wondered whether his caring father persona was an act. Face it. The trust she'd once had in him, and their marriage, had disappeared.

"I don't think that's the problem with Cassidy." Kate had the baby monitor on but heard no noise.

"She's lost her parents, spends her days at one house, and her nights at another. That's a lot of change for a baby."

Too much? Guilt slithered up her spine.

Jared wiped his mouth with a napkin. "She might feel better now that we're all here together."

Kate's muscles knotted. They were only together until Sunday, and then the situation would change. Again. "One can hope."

"Yes, one can." Mischief glinted in his gaze. "Where am I sleeping tonight?"

His suggestive tone made her set her cup on the counter before her unsteady hand dropped it. "You're in the guest bedroom."

Jared said nothing, but his eyes darkened. He shouldn't be surprised. Upset, perhaps. But this was what they'd agreed upon. The rules they'd set.

Ones they would follow. No matter what.

She expected him to say something, but he didn't. The silence magnified the stress between them. Kate wanted to fix that.

"I had the room cleaned out, including the armoire." She refilled his mug, hoping her words didn't sound as awkward as she felt. "I hung pictures on the wall, too."

As if Jared would care.

He took another bite of his sandwich.

"All you're missing is a dresser." She wanted to keep the silence from returning. "We can buy one this weekend."

His gaze focused on her, and her pulse skittered. "You've thought of everything."

The tone of his voice told her he hadn't meant the words as a compliment. "I, um, tried."

Because that was what Kate did—considered the possibilities, made plans for the contingencies, or at least she had until...tonight.

Jared had thrown her for a loop. And that left her worried about what the rest of the weekend would hold.

She might need that shot of whiskey.

Or better yet, an entire bottle.

* * *

So much for there being no place like home. Right now, being home sucked. Jared's new room was small—ten by ten if he were generous—without a closet.

Without his wife.

His feet hung off the full-size mattress. Jared glanced at the clock.

Midnight.

Sleep wasn't easy to come by when his wife, the woman he hadn't slept with in two months and twenty-three days, was in the room down the hall. Alone. In a king-size bed. Probably wearing a short nightshirt that had ridden up her thighs. He missed touching her soft skin and having her warm body pressed against his in a perfect fit.

As he calculated ways to make Kate fall for him again, his eyelids grew heavy. He'd been on East Coast time all week, and the three-hour difference was catching up to him. He rolled over, hoping sleep came hard and fast.

A cry shattered the silence of the house like a rooster's call at dawn.

He glanced at the clock. Two. The middle of the night.

Another cry.

Cassidy.

He scrambled out of bed, hit his calf on his luggage, and hurried to her room.

Kate had beat him there, and she held the baby.

A small lamp provided a dim light, enough for him to see them. As he imagined, Kate's nightshirt showed off her long, slender legs.

"Let's get you a bottle, hungry girl," she said.

Hungry girl. If only his wife were hungry for him.

The baby sobbed.

He concentrated on the task at hand. "Want some help?"

Kate sucked in a sharp breath. "I didn't hear you come in."

"Sorry." He yawned. "I'll get the bottle?"

"I can do it." But instead of heading to the kitchen, she lowered the fussing baby to the changing table and pulled a diaper from the lower shelf.

"Let me change her," he offered, not wanting to replay the scene earlier tonight. "While you warm the bottle."

Kate unzipped Cassidy's pajamas.

"If we work together," he said. "We can get back to bed that much sooner."

Alone, together, he'd take what he could get at this hour.

"Cassidy needs to be changed." Kate strapped the baby to the table and handed him the diaper. For a moment, they both held on to it, and then she looked away. "Everything is here, including a new sleeper if the one she's wearing is wet. I'll get a bottle."

Victory.

She was letting him help.

He undid the diaper, and his satisfaction evaporated.

Jared scrunched his nose.

Gross. He should have opted for the bottle.

After the diaper change, he rocked, swayed, and walked Cassidy, but nothing made the baby happier or sleepy.

Kate returned. "I can take her."

"You've done this all week." Jared reached for the bottle, purposely brushing his fingers against Kate's and watching her pull her hand away. She must have felt the heat, the connection, too. *Good.* He placed the bottle in an eager Cassidy's mouth. "Go to bed."

"Are you sure? She doesn't go right to sleep."

"All the more reason for you to grab some shut-eye now."

Kate bit her lip. "Yell if you need me."

He needed her. Badly. But not in the way she was offering. At least she hadn't argued with him. A positive step. "I will."

With that, she left the room. He pictured her crawling into bed, sliding under the covers and her nightshirt riding up again. One peek was all he wanted.

Jared glanced at Cassidy, who sucked down the formula as if it were a chocolate milkshake. "Let's see if you need to burp."

Once she'd burped, finished the bottle, and burped again, he walked Cassidy to her crib. She fussed, tears falling from her eyes. "Do you want to rock?"

She answered him with a sigh.

He sat on the rocker he'd helped Brady refinish. Cassidy settled for about five minutes until she cried again. Jared circled the room, and that seemed to do the trick until he stopped. The crying started again.

Now he understood what Kate had been talking about and why she looked exhausted. How had she done this every night without losing it? This was his first time, and he was tired of the routine and ready to sleep himself.

"It's late, baby." He walked like a robot on automatic mode, but the movement calmed Cassidy.

"You drank your bottle. Your diaper's clean. Time for nighty-night."

But the baby didn't understand. Or maybe she didn't care. He respected Kate dealing with this and still managing to go to work each morning.

"I'll take over," a quiet voice said from behind him.

"Kate," he said, surprised. "I thought you were asleep."

"I was but I woke up."

He wouldn't accept defeat. Those rings under her eyes seemed darker. Jared wondered if she'd slept. And that upset him. She never wanted to give up control. "I can do this."

"I know, but tomorrow will be a long day if we're both tired." She reached for the baby, but he didn't let go.

For a moment, the three of them were locked together. Not quite a group hug, or passionate in any sense of the word, but he would take it.

"Really, Jared, get some sleep."

He recognized the familiar determination in her voice.

Stalemate.

He couldn't count the number of times it had happened before. Arguing would lead to a fight.

Jared let go. "I won't sleep knowing you're awake."

She shrugged. "Then stay up. It's your choice."

THE HUSBAND

As he walked to the opposite side of the room and leaned against the wall, Kate sang a quiet lullaby. Funny, but he'd never heard her sing except one time at karaoke. Her voice, however, was different.

Love filled the sweet sound. Patience, too.

Her song captivated him, as did Kate herself.

She was a mom. Cassidy's mom.

They'd made the right choice for the baby. Jared had no doubt. He also knew something else. He needed Kate and Cassidy in his life. They were a family.

Kate didn't realize it yet, but she would. He would show her how much she needed him, stupid rules or not.

Chapter Thirteen

Cassidy usually woke at six o'clock in the morning. Today, with Jared in the house, Kate wanted to be prepared.

At five thirty, she showered and dressed, putting on gray pants, a pale pink blouse, a silver necklace, and matching earrings. She brushed a mineral powder foundation over her face before adding a touch of blush and lip gloss. Early for a Saturday, but walking around in her nightshirt didn't seem like a smart idea, especially after Jared had checked out her legs last night. Thank goodness she'd shaved.

Not that she wanted him to find her attractive.

Kate didn't.

But knowing her legs still appealed to him brought relief.

At precisely six o'clock, she sneaked a peek into the nursery. The sight of an empty crib sent panic rolling through her. She struggled to breathe. "Cassidy."

"Downstairs," Jared called up.

Kate hurried to the first floor and into the kitchen. She skidded to a stop.

Cassidy sat in her high chair, and Jared fed her from a bowl.

Kate's blood pressure spiraled. "What are you doing?"

"I'm feeding her breakfast."

"She's not eating solids yet."

"I found rice cereal in the pantry."

Kate placed her hands on her hips. "Your sister gave the box to your mother to give to me."

"I know," he said. "My mom told me."

"You called your mother?" As soon as the question was out, Kate realized how stupid her words must sound. He talked to his family all the time. His parents, his sisters, and brothers. Aunts, uncles, and cousins, too.

"Yes, I called her. The bottle didn't seem to be enough." Jared spooned more cereal into the baby's mouth. "Don't worry. After I talked with my mom, I double-checked the baby book on the counter. Solids are okay for her age."

"But they don't recommend starting solids until six months to alleviate allergies."

"Well, my mom fed us solids at four months, and we turned out okay." Jared stuck another spoonful of rice cereal into the baby's open mouth. "Besides, Cassidy likes it. She might sleep longer with something more substantial in her stomach."

If they wanted to be perfect parents, they needed to stick to a plan. Not make changes as it suited them. "You should have asked me first. I was awake."

"You were in the shower. I didn't think you'd appreciate me coming in there."

Okay, Jared was correct about that. Still… "You could have waited."

"Why? We're both Cassidy's guardians. Her parents, now. I realize you like things a certain way, and you've spent more time with the baby than I have, but I need to be a part of this, too."

"You are."

"Am I?" He raised a brow. "You could have slept last night and left Cassidy with me, but you didn't."

Okay, Kate would give him that one. "You were tired but stayed up, too."

"I'm only here two nights a week." He wiped Cassidy's messy face with her bib.

"A wet washcloth would work better."

He glared at her. "This is what I'm talking about."

"What?" Kate needed to defend herself. "I'm trying to help. And I wanted to wait until Cassidy was six months to try solid foods because Susan had a peanut allergy. Cassidy might be more susceptible to food allergies."

"I didn't know."

Not much of an apology, but knowing Jared, that was all Kate would get.

"If you're worried about allergies, we don't have to feed her anything else except rice cereal until she turns six months," he added.

She didn't want to fight. They'd argued too much before they broke up. "I guess."

"If it's any consolation, Cassidy's scarfing down the cereal like it's ice cream." He made a face. "Don't know why. The stuff tastes bland."

"You tried it?"

He nodded. "Isn't that what a parent is supposed to do?"

"I have no idea, but I've never seen that in the baby books."

"You should stop relying on the books."

Hurt flashed through her. Jared had his family to call for help, but with their strange marriage arrangement, she hadn't been comfortable doing the same. His family did enough caring for Cassidy during the week. Besides, Kate didn't want to appear incompetent. "And do what instead?"

He raised a brow. "Try winging it."

The concept went against Kate's instincts. "I'm not sure that's a good idea."

Cassidy knocked the spoon away with her hand.

Rice cereal flew and landed on Jared's face.

The baby squealed.

"Hilarious, sweet pea." Laughing, he wiped his eyes with a napkin. "At least the baby seems to understand the definition of winging it."

Kate wanted to remain indifferent to him and not care what he did or said. But at this moment, indifference was the last thing she felt for Jared. Especially when he looked so adorable with splotches of cereal and a dimpled smile on his face. "You look—"

"Like a clown?"

"No."

"A paper mâché model?"

"Close, but no, you look like a dad." She grabbed a paper towel, wet it, and wiped his face clean. "The kind who all the kids in the neighborhood will want to play with."

"What about you?"

She swallowed. "Me?"

"Would you want to play, too?"

Oh, yes. Kate met his warm, intent gaze, her heart thudding.

Oh, no.

* * *

Winging it worked great, Jared thought smugly a few hours later. As they walked the street full of cozy bungalows and English-style cottages on the partially cloudy May morning, Cassidy fell asleep in her stroller without so much as a peep. They might have finally learned the secret to naptime—keep the baby away from the crib.

"So...Chinese takeout, barbecue, or pizza for dinner?" Kate asked.

"Whatever's easiest," he said.

Being with her like this reminded him of when they'd first gotten married and walked through the tree-lined sidewalks holding hands and catching up on their week. Except this afternoon, they pushed a stroller, kept their distance from each other, and avoided any source of controversy with their conversation topic. No work talk, only food.

"Pizza would be the easiest," she said after they'd discussed various restaurants. "Pepperoni and mushroom."

His favorite.

"Don't you like olives and sausage?" he asked. "On a thick crust?"

She nodded. "But you prefer thin."

They were trying so hard to get along. Too hard?

He understood the reasoning. If they were polite, they could pretend no underlying passion and heat brewed between them. Maybe he should admit he was too tired to do anything but be a good boy and follow the rules. "Let's order a regular crust."

"Sounds good."

That wasn't enough for him. Jared wanted things back to the way they were. Even though they were outside, the atmosphere, like the conversation, was forced and strained. He didn't like that. But focusing on the negatives wouldn't help. The bottom line— they were together. They were a family. Perhaps not a totally functional one, but this had to be enough for now.

He noticed an empty lot on the corner. "What happened to the Piersons' house?"

"Someone tore it down. The land was worth more than the structure."

On that intersection alone, a house was for sale, a second had been demolished, another was being remodeled, and a fourth had been primed for a paint job.

"Things are changing," Jared said. "I've noticed more traffic from nonlocals."

"True. There are more cars on the streets, but our property value has gone up." She sounded pleased. "It's that old saying—location, location, location."

"I always thought the location was great."

"Now, others agree with you." Kate's mood seemed to improve. "A remodel would make financial sense. It would give us more space, another bathroom, and an updated kitchen."

Those improvements would increase resell value, but… "We should hold off. Too many changes at one time—"

"Would be too much," she finished for him.

There it was again—that sense of oneness. Strain,

stress, whatever else that kept them apart didn't hide the bond between them. She *had* to be aware of the connection, too.

"Plus, it's not ideal to spend the money since you just moved," Kate added, hurt sounding in her voice.

Jared squirmed. She made it sound like he'd abandoned her, which, in a way, he had. But he hadn't thought the separation would be forever. Just long enough to make her see she should move with him.

Only that hadn't happened.

Guilt over leaving and wanting them both to live in Seattle left a bitter taste in his mouth. Kate, however, failed to understand moving away from Portland wasn't only about him and his job. The larger city offered a bigger market. Her company would thrive there, and so would she. He just needed to convince her of that.

While Kate fixed lunch, Jared read board books to the baby. After lunch, they played with Cassidy under her floor gym. Sure, tension remained between him and Kate, but nothing had gone wrong as far as the baby was concerned. No need to refer to any books or turn to the Internet or his family. He and Kate were getting parenting down, and that sent pride rushing through him.

"It's afternoon naptime." He held Cassidy on his lap. "My mom says the baby takes two naps at her house."

"Why don't we take her on another walk?" Kate

suggested. "She can fall asleep, and we'll get exercise."

"You said she was dealing with a bunch of changes. We should keep to her routine at my parents' house."

"You're right."

Her dubious tone made him smile. He rose, ready for the challenge. "Then let's do it."

"I can put her down."

"So can I."

Impasse. Again.

Only this time, Jared held the prize. That meant he won. "Since I've got her, I'll put her down."

"I've got you covered."

He laughed. "You sound like we're going to war."

"Don't you remember last night?"

"It wasn't that bad." He carried Cassidy upstairs. "It's time for your nap, baby. Show us how well you can go to sleep on your own."

The baby gooed.

"That's right," he said. "Show us how tired you are, sleepyhead."

Kate followed him. "I wouldn't talk too much or get her excited."

"So, I shouldn't tickle her toesies?"

"I don't recommend it."

He shot her a smile. "What about yours?"

"Well"—her mouth curved—"this probably isn't the best time."

But she hadn't said no. Progress.

"Right now, we should put the baby to bed," Kate said.

Jared changed Cassidy's diaper and then kissed the top of her head, just above the white bandage. "Sleep well, Princess."

Mommy and Daddy need alone time.

He laid the baby in the crib. Wide-eyed and innocent, she gazed up at him with her big blue eyes, and she wailed. The bloodcurdling scream made every single nerve ending stand at attention like Buckingham Palace guards.

"Pick her up," Kate said, rushing to the crib.

"No." He patted Cassidy's shoulder. "We're here, baby, but you need to sleep."

The baby's face turned red, and tears shot from her eyes.

As Kate clutched the crib rail, her knuckles turned white. "This isn't working for me."

Him, either. "Give it—"

"Shhh." She picked up the baby. "Don't cry, sweetie. We're here."

A minute.

Cassidy rested her head on Kate's shoulder, held on to Kate's hair with one hand, and cried. "I can't let her cry. She has no idea where her parents are. I won't let her think they abandoned her. Susan wouldn't want that."

The minutes passed slower than the concession lines on opening day. With every tear the baby shed,

Jared's composure unraveled. After a half hour of the baby's tantrum, he wanted to scream himself.

"I can't take this much longer," he said finally.

"I know, but I'm not sure what else to try."

Swaying hadn't worked. Rocking, either.

He had to give Kate credit. Her voice remained calm. She kept in constant motion even though she looked ready to fall asleep at any minute.

"We've got to figure this out and make her stop." Before Cassidy's naptime behavior pushed them over the edge. They had enough problems on their own to work out. They didn't need this, too. "I'm going downstairs."

"For what?" she asked.

"To check the baby books."

Kate sat on the rocking chair for the third time. She arched her eyebrows, but her smile was sympathetic. "What happened to winging it?"

He shrugged. "So, I'm an idiot."

"No, you're a new parent, that's all," she said with the understanding of a mom. "It's not as easy as you think it will be."

"I don't know how you managed on your own."

"You do what you have to do."

Exactly. And Jared wouldn't let a tiny baby defeat them. A man on a mission, he stormed downstairs. As he thumbed through the stack of books on the table, he ran through the checklists with flowcharts and what-if scenarios. Nothing explained why Cassidy hated going to sleep so much. Nothing told him what to do. He contacted the pediatrician they'd been referred to, and the doctor on call recommended a children's pain reliever in case the mattress put pressure on her head. But even after that had time to work, the crying continued.

So he did what any other man would do in this situation. He called his mom.

"I don't know what the problem is, dear," his mother of five and grandmother of seven said. "Cassidy never makes a peep during her naps in the morning and the afternoon here. Have you checked her temperature?"

Jared disconnected from the call, ready to throw his cell phone. Instead, he returned to Cassidy's room. "Where's the thermometer?"

Kate walked back and forth with the baby in her arms. "She's not warm."

"Just tell me where it is."

She patted a sobbing Cassidy. "In the hall bathroom. Second drawer."

A minute later, he ran the probe over the unbandaged portion of her forehead, but the reading was way too low. What little remained of his tired spirits disappeared.

"Hold the button down as you scan," Kate explained kindly. "You'll hear beeps when it's finished."

"Thank you." Jared hoped he sounded sincere,

not irritated like he felt. None of this was Kate's fault. She was trying to help him—the way he wanted to help her.

He scanned the baby's forehead again, and this time the device worked. The action, however, aggravated Cassidy more, but he kept going. If her temperature was high, they could fix that. After the beeps, he checked the readout. His entire body sagged. "No fever."

A good thing, really, but that meant he had to keep searching for the reason she acted this way.

"What do you want to try next?" Kate asked.

"I've got nothing." Jared patted her shoulder. "I said it before, but I still can't believe you handled this yourself during the week."

"I only had to deal with nighttime, not naptime."

That was enough. And it earned his undying respect and admiration. "I'm still impressed."

"Thanks."

"So, do you have any other ideas?"

She gave a half smile. "Are you up for another walk?"

Chapter Fourteen

As they trekked around the neighborhood, Kate remained quiet. She didn't want to give the baby any reason to stay awake. Jared stayed silent, too. By the time they reached the end of the block, Cassidy slept soundly in her stroller. That gave Kate hope they would figure out how to parent sooner rather than later.

"Good call." Jared kept his voice low. "She's out."

"The question will be for how long."

A car drove passed them, and the driver who lived across the street waved.

"I enjoy being outside like this." He pushed the stroller. "I should take more walks."

Spring often brought rain showers, but the

weather was lovely for getting outside. Something she rarely did herself. But spending time with him was nice, too. Not that she would be comfortable admitting that. "Yes."

"And being together."

Not trusting her voice, she nodded.

"We've got this," he encouraged.

"We do." Because there wasn't any other option for them.

But at nine o'clock that night, Kate realized they'd been fooling themselves. Once again, Cassidy threw a tantrum. She didn't want to go to bed. It was too dark for another walk. Not that Kate had the inclination or the energy to take the baby out once more. Thank goodness Jared was here because Cassidy had pushed Kate over the edge.

Physically exhausted and emotionally drained, she collapsed on her bed.

How had Susan done this?

Her friend had mentioned being tired or wanting to lose weight, but she'd never complained about Cassidy. And that was all Kate had wanted to do today.

"We should wave the white flag and surrender!" she yelled to Jared, who walked the baby down the hallway. "That might make her stop crying."

Though Kate doubted it. She crawled under the covers. Too bad the cotton blanket wouldn't shield her from the latest fit. She'd do anything for a reprieve.

Cassidy sobbed.

Jared walked into the room and sat on the bed. "We're reaching the saturation stage."

The baby hiccupped.

The fatigue of trying to get Cassidy to sleep made Kate lightheaded. "I'll take over, but I'll need help to get up."

"Mind if we join you instead?" Jared asked.

The idea of staying in bed sounded divine. As Kate stared at the ceiling, she patted the space next to her. "Please do."

He placed the baby in the center of the king-size bed, so Cassidy lay between them. "Why don't we rest for a bit?"

Rest. The word was ambrosia to Kate's ears. Until she realized she'd invited Jared into her bed. Her body tensed.

What had she been thinking? She hadn't. That was the problem.

She bit her lip, trying to control her erratic pulse.

"That means you, too, baby," he said.

Cassidy's tears stopped as if she realized she'd won another round, and she cooed.

The baby.

Kate's worry was premature. Cassidy would keep anything from happening between her and Jared. Of course, if Kate stuck to the rules, nothing would happen anyway.

"She likes this bed," Jared said. "Just not her own."

"I don't understand." Kate rolled on her side, so she faced the now content baby and a relieved Jared. "How could this cute baby girl also be the crying crib monster?"

Cassidy reached into the air with her arms and kicked her yellow-footie-clad feet.

He laughed. "I don't know, but she's happy."

"Yes." Kate wanted to be happy, too, but she was...stressed. Especially the way Jared's shirt tightened across his chest and the muscles on his arms as he lay on his side. She swallowed.

Peals of laughter escaped from the baby's mouth.

"This beats tears." Kate tried to sound cheerful and not stare at him.

"Too bad it's not always like this."

He meant Cassidy. He had to mean Cassidy.

Kate wet her lips. "Perhaps we've reached a crossroad."

His gaze locked on hers. "I hope so."

Jared reached across the pillows and touched Kate's head.

She stiffened, unsure what to say, but knowing she shouldn't allow him to touch her. Not like this. In bed. Together.

He combed his fingers through her hair, and her body went limp. His touch felt so good and so right. That was so wrong. But Kate pushed aside logic and the reasons she should stop him. She wanted to enjoy this a few minutes longer.

All these months sleeping alone, she'd forgotten how good it was having him in bed with her. Kate almost sighed. "If you keep that up, I'll fall asleep."

"That will make two of you," he whispered.

The sight of Cassidy's closed eyes and curved lips brought relief.

Finally. Quiet.

"What if she wakes up?" Kate whispered, watching the baby's steady breaths.

He placed a pillow between their knees. "With you blocking that side and me on this side and the pillow down there, Cassidy can't go anywhere."

That meant Jared was staying, too. So many buts and what-ifs ran through Kate's mind. She was too tired to deal with them. Maybe in the morning they'd set new rules to deal with situations like this, but for now, she'd go with it.

Jared leaned over the baby and brushed his lips across Kate's. "Sleep well."

The kiss was platonic—a gesture out of camaraderie. Saying good night, that was all he'd been doing. She shouldn't read anything into the action.

Too bad her throbbing lips hadn't gotten that memo. She forced herself not to touch them.

"Close your eyes, Kate."

She did, but that didn't stop the thoughts running through her head.

"Night, Katie."

Kate cleared her dry throat. "Good night, Jared."

* * *

Except for sleeping in his own bed last night—albeit with Cassidy between him and Kate—the rest of the weekend didn't improve. Cassidy, a teeny, helpless baby, turned into a raging, demanding demon any time the crib was involved. Naptime and bedtime became battles. And Cassidy, by sheer willpower alone, had been victorious.

Kate didn't want Cassidy to get in the habit of sleeping with her, and Jared agreed. He wanted to be the only person in bed with Kate.

But a person could only take so many walks, and by Sunday night, Jared felt like a war zone refugee—sleepless, homeless, shell-shocked. He couldn't wait to return to Seattle, though he would miss Kate. His job, even during the most critical of times, had never been as hard as taking care of a baby. He was ready for R & R.

One good thing had come out of the baby battles—he and Kate had become a team, trying to get the baby to go to sleep without a World War III reaction.

Jared hated leaving her alone to deal with Cassidy. Kate was exhausted when he arrived. His visit had barely given her a respite. How would she survive another week of the Crib Demon routine on her own?

He watched Cassidy play under her floor gym. "I'm sorry I have to go."

"You have your job," Kate said evenly. "I understand."

Her understanding increased his guilt. "We have to do something about Cassidy."

"I know." Frustration clouded Kate's pretty face. "She never does this at your parents' house."

"That's what my mom told me."

"Cassidy needs more consistency."

"Consistency?"

"If Cassidy spent more time here during the day so this isn't only the place she comes to for a bottle, bath, and bedtime, she might not have such a terrible reaction each night."

"An excellent theory, but my parents won't want to spend their days here."

"No, you're right."

He hated to see her so discouraged. "You mentioned a leave of absence the other day."

"Yes, but I can't do that. I'm still trying to catch up from the time I spent in Boise." She bit her lip. "Things would fall apart."

Things were falling apart. If she didn't sleep, if Cassidy didn't settle into her new home, Kate would make herself sick.

He studied her. "At the office, you mean."

She stuck out her chin. "Yes."

He should have known. Her career came first. Before her health, before their marriage, before Cassidy.

But that was unfair. His job came first, too.

Lots of new moms worked by choice or necessity. Kate was doing her best to juggle a demanding job during the day with a demanding baby during the night. She was doing more than he was.

Jared took a deep breath. "Kate, you can't go on like this."

A lengthy silence ensued.

"I'll be fine," she said. "I just need to quit running every time Cassidy makes a sound."

Kate sounded confident, and her plan made sense. But he didn't believe her. Ordinarily, Jared would take Kate at her word and take off, but this time...he didn't want to leave.

He stared at his two girls. Something had to change or the happy future, the perfect family he was striving for was never going to happen. He needed to step up to the plate and hit the grand slam. "I'll take time off from work and stay home with Cassidy."

Kate's mouth gaped. "What?"

"I haven't looked at what my company offers for family leave, but since it won't be for long, I might as well use vacation time and get paid." Jared couldn't believe he was doing this, but what choice did he have if he wanted to do what was best for his family? "That should help Cassidy adjust quicker."

Kate stuck her tongue between her teeth. "You'd do that for the baby?"

"Not just for the baby. For you, too. And me," he

added hastily when her mouth tightened. Kate never accepted his help. "I'd worry about you here alone."

"That's thoughtful of you, but I've managed so far."

"You've done great, but remember what I said. We're in this together. I mean that, Kate."

Gratitude filled her eyes. That told him he was making the right decision.

"I still must be in Seattle tomorrow morning, but it should be a quick trip. Two or three days at most. They managed without me while I was in Boise. They can survive another week or two." Jared kept his voice steady when he had no idea what his boss would say. "I've accrued so many weeks of vacation. I don't think I've used any since our honeymoon and last week."

Which, thinking about it, was a sad statement about his life. And their marriage.

She looked wistful. "There wasn't enough—"

"Time," he finished for her. "Remember Maui?"

She nodded. "How could I forget? We were at the airport, ready to go."

And as quickly as that, the tentative rapport between them faded as old hurts, old conflicts surfaced. "I told you to turn off your cell phone," he said.

"How was I to know my biggest client had been slapped with a class-action lawsuit?"

"You wouldn't have known if you'd listened to me."

"I would have had to fly back, anyway."

"You could have allowed someone else to handle the situation."

"Situation? It was a crisis. My firm's reputation was on the line. I couldn't hand the client off to someone else and go on vacation." She brushed her hair behind her shoulder. "At least I got us a refund, unlike the trip to Cancun."

"Hey, I had no choice but to fly to New York. Boss's orders. We were supposed to reschedule the trip, but then..."

"We never did."

And probably never would. Jared swallowed.

"There won't be time in the future for big vacations, so I might as well use the time now," he said. "As long as you don't mind me being here during the week, too."

"I won't mind you here," she said softly, making him wonder if she was having a change of heart about the two of them.

He hoped so. "I'll try not to get in your way."

They used to joke about being two planes passing in the night. Except for the week of Thanksgiving and the time between Christmas and New Year's, they rarely spent weeknights together because of travel schedules. At least they would only work around one job now.

A stay-at-home dad.

Temporarily, he assured himself. Just until they

tamed the Crib Demon, and he made sure Kate ate and slept. He would relieve her of the bedtime battles and make the next move in his game plan to win her back. He would quadruple the progress he'd made so far.

"I'll talk to my boss first thing in the morning," Jared said.

"You being here will be good for Cassidy."

His being here would be great for all three of them. Kate would realize that soon enough. Game face on, he clapped his hands together. "Just call me Mr. Mom."

She smiled. "Somehow, I never pictured us as Mr. Mom and Mrs. Dad."

"What about Mr. and Mrs. Jared Reed?" he challenged.

Her smile faded. "I don't think so."

"So, what do you suggest?"

"Hmmm." She pressed her lips together and winked. "What about Mr. and Mrs. Kate Malone?"

Chapter Fifteen

Wednesday evening, Kate pulled into her driveway. Lights shone through the window. That meant Jared was there.

A strange mix of apprehension and relief flowed through her.

She parked the new four-door SUV crossover in front of the garage that housed her beloved silvery-blue BMW Boxster and turned off the engine. But she remained in the car.

These past two and a half days without Jared had been horrible. Bedtime with Cassidy had only worsened since he'd left on Sunday. But knowing he would be here for at least a week made Kate nervous and uncertain. He'd been nothing but cooperative, trying to make this arrangement work, but she hated unpredictability. She hated not having control. And that was what she feared would happen with him here.

Cassidy squealed.

Kate glanced in the mirror. The baby's smiling face reflected off another attached to the back seat. Affection overflowed. Surely doing what Susan desired for her daughter would make Kate's struggles worthwhile. "Give me a minute, okay?"

The baby cooed.

She would take that as a yes.

As she spotted Jared in the kitchen, fluttery sensations overtook her stomach. She clutched the steering wheel. The butterfly aviary inside her had nothing to do with apprehension, and everything to do with attraction.

Uh-oh. Maybe that was the actual problem—the temptation of having him around 24/7 and what that might bring.

A bed-size lump of worry lodged in her throat.

She couldn't afford to be tempted. She didn't want to upset the precarious relationship—make that situation—between them. Too much was at stake.

She glanced in the mirror at Cassidy.

The baby deserved to have both a mother and a father.

Which meant Kate needed to encase her heart in armor to make it immune from Jared. From his good looks and witty charm, from his willingness to use his vacation time to care for a child he hardly knew, and to help his almost-but-not-quite-ex-wife transition from working woman to working mother.

She exhaled slowly.

Cassidy giggled, another pleasant sound, but Kate wouldn't push the baby's cheerful mood. She didn't want tears to start Jared's second homecoming. That would happen soon enough when bedtime rolled around.

She exited the car, swung her laptop case strap over her shoulder, and opened the back door. "Are you ready to get out?"

"Ah-goo," Cassidy said.

Kate repeated the sound. "That's your favorite word, isn't it?"

"Ah-goo."

"Let's go." She reached into the center of the back seat and then carried Cassidy to the door that opened as if on cue.

The scents of basil and garlic drifted out.

Oh, that smelled delicious.

Her stomach growled. She hadn't eaten a proper meal with the five food groups or drank a liquid without a heavy dose of caffeine since...Sunday. When Jared had been here last.

"Perfect timing," he announced as she stepped inside. "Dinner's almost ready."

"You cooked?"

A silly question once she saw the kitchen. A red

liquid simmered in a pan on the stove. An empty pasta sauce jar, a bag of spaghetti noodles, and a bottle of Chianti sat on the counter. Water boiled in an enormous pot. Something—garlic bread, she hoped—baked in the oven.

As Kate set her briefcase on the floor, she recalled what she'd given him when he'd arrived last Friday evening—a cold sandwich—but cooking for him hadn't entered her mind. Of course, Jared hadn't been taking care of a baby while trying to fix dinner tonight, and she'd done the best she could. But she probably should have had a hot meal prepared for him. That was what a perfect wife would have done. Perhaps if she'd done more things like that when they were married, he wouldn't have left her and moved to Seattle.

"It smells delicious." Her nervousness in the car now seemed paranoid. He'd cooked her dinner, not tried to seduce her. She glanced at the bottle of wine. No, she had nothing to worry about as long as he didn't offer to rub her back. Kate cleared her throat. "When did you get here?"

"Around three." He dumped the bag of pasta into the boiling water and set the timer on the stove. "My boss wanted me in on a conference call this morning."

"Is he okay with you taking vacation time?"

Jared nodded. "He asked me to check in with him at the end of the week. I told him I'd probably be away for two weeks."

Two weeks. She could handle that if he could. A bottle sat in the warmer. "For Cassidy?"

"It should be ready."

Kate switched the baby to her left side before testing the temperature of the formula. Perfect. She shouldn't be surprised. Not with the competence he'd showed tonight. "Thanks. You've thought of everything."

He smiled. "I gave it my best shot."

She sat at the kitchen table—set with plates, silverware, napkins, and wineglasses—and fed the bottle to a hungry Cassidy. Kate had no idea what she'd expected when she walked in the door, but this—a scene out of an alternate reality 1950s television show—wasn't it.

Jared stirred the sauce with a wooden spoon.

A satisfied grin formed on her lips. Sure, he'd only cooked dinner, but the caring gesture made her feel special. Cherished. A way she hadn't felt in a long time. And she liked it.

"Do you need any help?" she asked.

"Thanks, but I'm almost done."

As the baby slurped her formula, Jared checked the boiling noodles, lowered the temperature on the bubbling sauce, and removed the bread baking from the oven. He'd always been comfortable cooking, more so than her, but she'd never seen him look so...domestic. He seemed perfectly at home in the kitchen.

Her kitchen.

Their kitchen, now.

Unfamiliar heat burned deep within Kate. She pressed her toes against the hardwood floor. "I could get used to this."

He glanced her way. "You think?"

Uh-oh. She hadn't meant to say the words out loud. She nodded when her answer was "most definitely." And that, Kate acknowledged, was a problem.

She wanted her and Jared to establish a stable home and a routine for Cassidy, but Kate would do the same for herself. She would only end up disappointed and heartbroken again. They'd agreed on a marriage of convenience, not a happily ever after.

She patted Cassidy's back, and a loud burp exploded from the baby.

"That's my girl." Jared stirred the sauce again. "You'll show up the boys when you are older."

His words sounded like something a dad would say, especially his dad. Kate fed the rest of the bottle to the baby. "Your parents didn't mention you were in town when I picked up Cassidy."

He sliced the garlic bread. "My parents don't know."

Kate fumbled with the baby's bottle. Jared told his family everything. Good news, bad news. Nothing was off-limits with the Reeds. "You haven't talked to them about this?"

"I want to speak to them in person. I'm telling them over breakfast tomorrow while you're at work."

That would spare her the inevitable recriminations. Kate appreciated that.

Dropping the baby off in the morning and picking her up in the evening had gotten easier. Her discussions with his parents and siblings revolved around Cassidy, but Kate was unsure of how to act around them.

She burped the baby again. "Are you concerned about their reactions?"

"My mom won't have a problem, but my dad..." Jared placed the bread on a plate and covered it with foil. "He may have some issues."

In other words, Vesuvius—the family nickname for his father's temper—would blow.

Even though Frank Reed was now retired, he remained a throwback to the days of a man who expected dinner at six o'clock on the dot no matter whether his wife, Margery, was fighting the flu, or chasing after her brood of grandchildren. Frank didn't understand why Kate hadn't moved to Seattle and had filed for divorce instead, so Jared taking over primary childcare duties would not go over well.

"What time are you heading over there?" Kate asked.

"I'm not." He dumped the pasta in a large bowl, poured the sauce on top, and stirred the mixture with the spoon. "I invited them to come here."

Here. Tomorrow. She gulped, making a mental note to clean the house tonight. His parents hadn't been here in months, and she wanted everything perfect for them. "Why here?"

He winked. "Home field advantage."

* * *

Forget home being any advantage. Jared's father wasn't swayed in the slightest.

Flipping pancakes on the stove, Jared realized cooking a meal for his dad while telling him he was staying home with the baby hadn't been a smart move.

"People will call you Mr. Malone." His father sneered. "I can't believe you're going to throw away an MBA and a six-figure income to change dirty diapers, do housework, and cook."

"Those are what I did and still do, Frank." His mother spoke before Jared could reply. She fed Cassidy another spoonful of rice cereal. "You had no complaints about me doing the same thing."

"You're a woman." His dad's nostrils flared. "That's your responsibility."

She shook her head. "Times have changed."

"Gah," Cassidy said.

"See." His mother smiled. "Cassidy agrees with me."

His dad harrumphed.

At least his mom was on Jared's side. She would talk sense into his father, but Jared wouldn't give up himself. He transferred the pancakes to a plate. "We have a housecleaner, so I won't scrub toilets or mop the floor. I also won't cook every night."

His dad grumbled under his breath. "It's abnormal for a man to stay home while his wife goes to work."

Jared carried the plate to the table.

His father frowned. "The next thing you know, he'll be wearing an apron."

"*He* is standing right here," Jared said. "Pancakes, anyone?"

"I'll take two more, son."

As Jared dished up the pancakes, he grimaced. His father might complain, but he wasn't above eating the food he'd cooked. Seconds, even.

"Don't forget, Dad." Jared sat at the table. "I didn't quit my job."

Though he'd lost a big opportunity with a longtime client by taking time off, he wouldn't tell his parents or Kate about that. Whatever sacrifices he made would be worth it when he and Kate were together, living as husband and wife.

His dad added a pat of butter to his pancakes. "Are you being paid?"

"Full salary and benefits." The only thing missing was marital benefits, but Jared would work on those. Starting tonight, if he got the chance.

"When do you return to your job?" his father asked.

"I don't know yet." Jared cut into his pancakes. "Probably two weeks."

The lines on his father's face deepened.

"Frank, this is a good thing," his mom encouraged. "We'll not only get to see Cassidy, but we'll get to see Jared, too."

"Does that mean you'll still bring her over?"

Jared nodded. "We want Cassidy to be comfortable at both places, but we need to establish a routine and get her used to sleeping in her crib first."

His dad leaned back in his chair. "Why don't you let the baby stay with us all the time?"

His mom laughed. "So, you can stay home all day with Cassidy, but not Jared?"

His father puffed out his chest. "I'm retired. I've earned my keep."

"Your father has fallen in love with this baby girl." His mother's tender gaze focused on Cassidy. "And so have I."

The attention his parents paid to Cassidy while she ate confirmed this. He wondered if they ever left her alone for a minute. They hadn't this morning. "We appreciate all you've done so far and will do for us after I go back to Seattle."

"You could stay home full-time," his mother suggested.

"Yeah, right," Jared and his dad said in unison.

His mom shook her head. "What does Kate think about all this?"

"I've only been here a day." Jared thought about Kate's reaction to his offer, her pleasure over the dinner last night, and her concerns about his father's response. Forward steps, definitely. "But the weekend was...encouraging."

And if she allowed him back in the master bedroom again, things would be even better.

His mom leaned forward, visibly curious about her children's lives, as usual. "So, the weekend went well?"

"'Well' might be a tad optimistic." He picked up his coffee cup. "It's hard to work on being a couple when our energy and time is spent on a baby who won't sleep, fusses, and cries when she should be sleeping."

His parents laughed.

"What?" Jared asked.

"Welcome to our world, dear." His mother's eyes twinkled. "Just multiply what you're going through by five."

"Is this what parenting will always be like?" He wasn't sure he wanted to hear the answer.

"They sleep eventually," his father said and then poured syrup over his pancakes.

"And cry less." His mom wiped a speck of cereal from Cassidy's chin. "But once you have kids, your world revolves around them. Finding time for romance, and each other, gets more difficult."

They'd had enough trouble before Cassidy arrived. Jared ate his pancake. Somehow, he and Kate needed to find time for each other.

"It helps to maintain your perspective, not to mention your sanity when you have a spouse who's there to share in all the ups and downs," his mom added.

He set his fork down. "I have Kate."

His parents both sipped from their coffee cups.

Their action put him on the defensive. Jared understood why they might feel like that—Kate had decided not to move to Seattle, and she had been the one to file for divorce. But those things must be forgotten. The sooner his family realized that, the better. "Kate and I are committed to raising Cassidy together."

"That's what you've said."

"We're going to forget about the divorce and make our marriage work," he added. At least that was the current plan. "Kate's withdrawing her dissolution petition as soon as she has time."

"Wonderful news. We only want you to be happy." His mom placed her cup on the table. "And we'll do whatever we can to help you."

But they didn't believe the marriage would work. The truth shone in his parents' eyes, and their skepticism pierced his heart. And that hurt. More than he wanted to admit. He would not fail.

Jared set his chin. "You'll see."

And they would.

Once Cassidy settled into a routine and Kate accepted his ongoing presence in their house, her bed, and life, they would have the kind of partnership, the kind of marriage, his parents were talking about. He only hoped it happened soon.

Chapter Sixteen

As Kate entered the living room that afternoon, Jared sat on the couch with the laundry basket at his feet. Cassidy played in the bouncer, sitting on the floor. On the bottom of the television screen, stock symbols rolled by on the electronic ticker tape.

If only Kate found the stock market interesting, she would concentrate on the trades scrolling by instead of taking in Jared's casual clothes—a green polo shirt, khaki shorts, and bare feet. He appeared relaxed. That made him even more attractive.

Her knees had shot past being wet noodles. They were at the Jell-O stage now.

She sucked in a breath. Not the reaction she'd hoped to have when she saw him.

Kate needed to focus on removing her shoes. As

she steadied herself by holding on to a chair, she kicked off her slingbacks. "Hi there."

Jared stopped folding a pink gingham crib sheet. Concern filled his gaze. "Why are you home so early?"

Good question. She wished she had an equally good answer. "I, um, let everyone have the afternoon off."

He tossed the bedding into the basket. "Are you sick?"

Funny, but several employees had asked the same thing. "I'm fine. Rested, too, since you took the middle-of-the-night shift."

She'd wondered whether his plan to stay home with Cassidy would work, but today had been near typical. After the panic and disarray of the last week and a half, the familiarity reassured Kate. She was more like her old self. Sean Owens, her dedicated assistant, had commented on her "return." She wouldn't deny the results—a pleasant and productive day, make that two-thirds of one, at the office.

"So why did you let everyone go home early?" Jared asked.

"Because I wanted to be here, not there." And see him and Cassidy. Kate never left work early unless she was catching a flight for a business trip. "I didn't want to leave unless everyone left, too."

"You're a great boss."

She wasn't sure if that was a compliment or not, but she was in too good a mood to let it get to her. She sat on the floor next to Cassidy. "Hello, baby, did you have a pleasant day?"

As drool rolled from the baby's mouth, Cassidy smiled.

Kate had made the right decision to come home early.

"Tell us what you did today," Jared said. "I'm in desperate need of adult conversation."

She glanced his way. Her heart went bumpity-bump.

"Kate?" he asked.

She spun the mirror on the baby bouncer much to Cassidy's delight. "We signed a new client, beBuzz Sportswear."

"Congrats."

"Thanks." Exhilaration washed over Kate. It was wonderful to share her accomplishment with someone other than her staff. She didn't have that many friends—Susan and two classmates from college. Most everyone else she'd met through Jared, and they'd taken his side when they broke up. "Today capped off a long and unsteady courtship."

"Sometimes, those are the most fruitful."

"I hope you're right."

"Me, too," he said, his intense gaze on her.

She wondered if he was talking about her new client or the two of them.

"We should open a bottle of champagne and celebrate," he added.

Glasses of bubbly might not be the smartest move when her eyes were glued on him. She remembered the last time they'd drunk champagne. Strawberries and whipped cream had been involved. "I was thinking about taking you and Cassidy to dinner."

Jared's surprised expression brought a rush of uncertainty. His lack of response intensified those feelings.

"Want to eat out tonight?" She kept her voice steady when her insides shook worse than those of a nervous schoolgirl asking a boy to a Sadie Hawkins dance. "Your choice of restaurant, but it's not like a date."

"That would be against the rules."

He still hadn't answered her question. She tilted her chin. "Yes, but we could, um, consider it practice. For, um, later, if we...when we see other—"

"I'd like to go," he interrupted to her relief. "But I'm not sure Cassidy will enjoy it. Why don't we have my parents watch her? We'd probably enjoy ourselves more."

"True. But we're supposed to be establishing a routine for the baby."

"You're right," he said, sounding disappointed.

"What if we wait until she goes to sleep?" Kate suggested.

"I'll call them." He picked up the phone and spoke to his mom. A minute later, he hung up. "They'll be here at seven."

"I hope getting her to fall asleep doesn't take hours."

"Cassidy napped twice in her crib today." Pride filled his voice.

"How did that happen?"

"My mom taught me the importance of a bedtime routine, not just a schedule, and something called a binky."

"A what?"

"A pacifier." Jared smiled. "She figured we used one since Cassidy took it so easily at her house."

Kate wracked her brain. "I don't remember if Susan used one."

"Would you have paid that close attention?"

"No, but I can't believe a pacifier made the difference."

"Not just the pacifier." He refolded the sheet. "But having a set routine we follow every time we put her down. I was skeptical myself, and she cried a little, but nothing like her never-ending Crib Demon crying fits."

"Excellent job."

A shy smile curved his lips. "My mom deserves credit. I only offered an assist."

"I'll thank her when she gets here. Speaking of which, how did this morning go with your parents?"

"They enjoyed the pancakes."

That didn't tell her much. "What did they think about you taking time off to be with Cassidy?"

And me, a little voice in Kate's head whispered.

"My mother supports my decision." He folded a

pink-trimmed dress. "She said I had evolved and become a man for the twenty-first century by putting the needs of my family ahead of my career goals."

"That's great."

Jared shrugged. "My dad wasn't as pleased."

He tried to sound lighthearted, but Kate knew how much his father's opinion meant to Jared. "I'm sorry."

"He'll get over it."

Of course his father would. Jared was the golden child, the son who never did wrong, never disappointed. Frank would never stay mad at him for long.

"If it's any consolation," she offered, "I agree with your mom. What you're doing for Cassidy is incredible."

Jared's gaze held hers, and she had to force herself to breathe. "Thanks."

Kate had done nothing to deserve his thankfulness. Not really. And that made her feel bad. Useless.

Cassidy reached up. "Gah."

"Are you ready to get out?" Kate looked at the baby dressed in a pink and yellow jumper and did a double take. She unhooked the strap holding the baby in the bouncer and lifted her out. "Did you and Cassidy go out today?"

"We walked to the store."

Kate's frustration rose. "Did she wear this?"

Jared studied the baby. "Is something wrong with

her clothes?"

Kate stifled a groan. "Her outfit is on backward."

"The snaps go in the front."

"In the back," she said.

"No, they don't."

"Yes, they do." She unsnapped the jumpsuit and showed him the tag. "They go in the back where this belongs, too."

Kate put the clothing on the baby the correct way. "See."

A beat passed.

"No wonder all those women kept staring at us in the produce department. I thought they were looking at me, not at Cassidy's clothing." Jared released a heavy sigh. "No doubt, they were whispering about my inability to dress my baby, not my remarkable pecs."

The humor in his voice evaporated her frustration. She laughed. "Okay, Cassidy wearing her outfit backward probably isn't a big deal."

He tilted his head. "You think?"

Kate nodded, hating that she almost ruined a pleasant afternoon. "Overreacting is my way of compensating for my lack of parenting skills and knowledge."

He feigned disbelief. "No."

"Yes." She stared at Cassidy's orange and blue socks. Not what she would have chosen to match the baby's pink shoes and clothing, but the little girl didn't have to coordinate from head to toe. At least not under Jared's watch. "I'll try harder."

"You already have. You're doing a fantastic job."

"Thanks." His compliment meant the world to her. Kate needed to hear she was doing well, even if it wasn't a hundred percent true. "I've been feeling like a lone wolf mom."

"You don't have to feel that way anymore, Katie," Jared said with a smile. "Daddy wolf is here to help."

"You taking the two a.m. wake-up last night was huge."

"Those are my specialty. I just have to keep my howling at the moon to a minimum."

She laughed. Cassidy did the same.

"I doubt the baby would mind the howling," Kate said. "She loves mimicking sounds and would howl alongside you."

"You're probably right."

He howled.

Cassidy released a high-pitched squeal.

"You don't have to worry about her when she's with me," Jared said seriously.

"I know." No matter how much Kate might want to run everything, doing so wouldn't be fair to him or good for their arrangement. They would both have to compromise for the marriage to work. "I won't interfere with what you do with Cassidy."

"And I'll do my best to dress her properly with the tag in the back." With a hopeful smile, he extended his arm. "Deal?"

Kate shook his hand. "Deal."

Chapter Seventeen

*D*eal?

The only deal Jared wanted to make with Kate was about her being his wife...for real. Sure, he should be patient. He'd only been in town one day. But each time he saw her, the pull grew stronger.

Now that she sat across from him with the candlelight flickering, he hated to deny what he wanted.

A waiter removed the plates from the linen-covered table.

"I'm glad we did this tonight," Kate said, looking more beautiful than ever. Her shimmery blue dress matched the color of her eyes.

It was a good thing they were out in public, or Jared might be in trouble. Who was he kidding? He was already in trouble.

She looked at him expectantly, waiting for his response.

"Me, too," he said.

Her hair tucked casually behind her ears made her appear younger, almost innocent. The smoldering heat in her eyes, however, was like a kick in the gut.

Couldn't she see their physical attraction wasn't the problem? It would solve their problems.

The air seemed electrified. Jared reached for his water glass. "We must do this again."

Yes. Anything to bring warmth to her smile and the radiant glow to her face.

Unless he found other ways of doing that. He grinned.

A spark of laughter danced in her eyes. "Especially if we can find another place as quiet as this one."

It wasn't church-quiet, but the soft conversation from the other diners seemed like whispers compared to Cassidy's chattering and crying. "You noticed that, too?"

She nodded.

"It's amazing how much noise a baby makes."

"Cassidy talks back to her bottle when she's drinking her formula," Kate said. "But I'm getting used to the racket."

That was good except… "I'll need a few more days before I can say the same."

"It won't be easy, and there will be a transition

period, but you'll get there, and things will be fine."

That was interesting. It sounded like his game plan for winning Kate back.

"I hope you know how much I appreciate you taking time off from work." She smiled shyly. "It's incredible what you're doing."

Her words made him feel ten feet tall, but he wanted to give credit to her, too. "You're the incredible one, Kate. I'm amazed at how much you've done with Cassidy. You can handle anything."

"I have a lot to learn, but thanks." Kate's eyes softened. "It's strange, but sometimes I think I hear her crying when I'm at work."

"That's not strange. You've changed."

"How?"

"Today, you gave your employees the afternoon off, and you came home early yourself. When was the last time that happened?"

"Never."

"I bet it won't be the last time." He saw his future: Kate, Cassidy, more babies. "You're a mom now, learning to be more flexible and not so set in your ways."

"Everything seems so different."

The anxiety in her voice, coupled with her sudden interest in the salt and pepper shakers, suggested she wasn't talking only about the baby. "What do you mean?"

"Tonight. Here, with you." She toyed with her

napkin. "I can't remember the last time we had a meal together in the middle of the week."

"Burgers in Boise."

"I meant at home. Before."

Before the separation.

Jared came up blank. Not surprising, given their schedules. "Dinner out on a Wednesday night is more satisfying than a call from a hotel room."

"I agree. We should make the most of the time while we can. Once you return to work..."

It would be back to phone calls.

He wanted to reassure her. And himself. "We'll figure something out. Video calling. You'll think I'm with you."

"Except, I'll be the one taking out the garbage."

"Builds muscles," he teased. "But I just arrived yesterday. Let's not think about me going away already."

The sommelier approached with two flutes containing champagne. "I hear you are celebrating a special occasion."

Jared nodded. "My wife is."

She gave him the arched eyebrow, what-are-you-doing look.

He leaned forward. "You never said no to champagne."

"But the baby—"

"Is asleep. My parents would have called if something was wrong. I only ordered us each a glass, not an entire bottle."

The sommelier waited patiently.

Kate smiled at the wine steward. "Thank you so much. A sip of celebratory bubbly would be lovely."

"My pleasure." The man placed the glasses on the table and bowed. "Enjoy."

Once the man walked away, Jared raised his champagne. "To a successful partnership."

"And a lasting one."

He hoped she wasn't only talking about her new client.

She tapped her flute against his. The chime of the crystal hung in the air like the song of a bird on a sunny day.

As she sipped, she seemed uncertain, a little nervous.

"Is something wrong?" he asked.

Her cheeks flushed. She set her glass down. "No."

He didn't believe her. Definitely a new Kate, and one he liked.

The waiter arrived with an order of profiteroles with two forks, a cappuccino for her, and a cup of decaf for him.

"These are my absolute favorite." She stared at the ice-cream-filled pastry puffs sprinkled with powdered sugar and drizzled with chocolate syrup. Jared wished she'd gaze at him with the same desire. "You're spoiling me."

That was the point. "I'm only getting started."

"Promises. Promises."

She would see it soon enough.

He scooped a bite onto his fork and lifted it toward her mouth. "For you."

Temptation flashed across her face, but caution tempered it. "I don't think this is such a good idea."

"The rules."

She nodded.

Screw the rules. Jared wanted to feed his wife.

"Come on, baby." He brought the fork closer. "Show me the tunnel so the choo-choo can come inside."

A relaxed smile formed. "It's a hangar, and the plane needs to go inside."

"Open up."

She did. He placed the bite into her mouth, and her lips closed around it. "Mmm."

Talk about sexy.

Slowly, he pulled the fork away. "Was it good for you?"

She laughed, the melodic sound wrapping around his heart. "Delicious."

He agreed.

A drop of chocolate sauce hung on her lower lip. As the pink tip of her tongue darted out to wipe it away, Jared's temperature skyrocketed. Sweet torture. He wanted a taste himself.

As Kate ate more, the waiter brought the check. Jared reached for the bill, but she was faster.

"It's my turn," he said.

When they used to go out, each took a turn paying.

"You can pay for the champagne and dessert," she said. "But I invited you. Dinner is my treat."

He didn't want to spoil the night by insisting on picking up the tab. With a shrug, he handed her cash to cover his portion. "Thank you for dinner, but I hope you know I'm not an easy date."

The corners of her eyes crinkled. "I'll try not to be too disappointed."

He cocked a brow. "But for you, I'm willing to make an exception."

Laughing, she placed her credit card inside the leather-covered folder. The waiter promptly took the bill away.

Kate ate another bite of the dessert and wiped her mouth. "Thank you for the dessert, Jared. And the champagne. I appreciate your support."

"You deserve it."

"Lots of people worked on winning the beBuzz account."

"I'm not only talking about your firm signing a client, Katie."

She glanced up. "What, then?"

"Cassidy."

"I'm doing what anyone else would do if their best friend died." Eyes glistening, she looked up and blinked. "Besides, Cassidy is easy to love. Even if she won't sleep at night."

Kate's humility touched him. He reached across the table and took hold of her hand, thin yet strong like the woman herself. "You've opened your heart and your life to the baby. You've become a mom. You've surprised me, my family, and no doubt everyone else you know."

She bit her lip. "I never said I didn't want children."

"No, you didn't," Jared admitted. "But saying you wanted a family and then putting off getting pregnant made me wonder."

"I'm sorry. I never meant to send mixed signals."

"Me, either." He squeezed her hand. "You're a wonderful mother and a beautiful, intelligent woman. I'm so proud you're my wife."

The gratitude shining in her eyes took his breath away.

The waiter returned with the bill. Kate pulled her hand from Jared's, and she filled out the charge slip. She placed the pen inside the folder and her napkin on the table.

"Finished?" he asked.

She nodded. "I'm ready to go home."

Home.

Their home.

Maybe tonight would be the turning point. The start of them having an actual marriage...

Anticipation rippled through him. If Kate desired him, that meant she still loved him.

He stood and pulled out her chair. As they exited the restaurant, he placed his hand on the small of her back. She didn't stiffen; her muscles didn't tense.

A good sign.

"Thank you, Jared. Tonight was…special. I want to do something in return."

"You can," he said.

"What?"

He unlocked the car, opened her door, and helped her into the seat. "You were never an easy date, either, but…"

Her eyes narrowed. "But what?"

With a grin, he walked to his side and slid into the car. "I wouldn't turn down a goodnight kiss."

"A kiss?" She didn't sound horrified. More…intrigued. "This isn't a real date."

Could've fooled him. He locked his seat belt into place. "Not a date kiss. A slow, hot, take-your-breath-away date kiss wouldn't be appropriate."

"Not appropriate at all." Kate shifted positions. "What kind of kiss do you mean?"

"A kiss between friends. That's all."

"To get us back in the game, so to speak."

"Exactly."

"Okay." She leaned over and kissed him lightly on the lips.

The fresh scent of her surrounded him, making him heady. Her mouth lingering an instant longer than he expected ignited a fire inside him. His boiling blood pushed him toward the edge. He was ready to jump. She only had to say the word.

"Friendly enough for you?" she asked with a slow, seductive smile. The woman didn't have an innocent bone in her body. Kate knew where she wanted him—and had him.

Jared cleared his throat. "Yes. Thank you."

He was back in the game, and so was she. Now all he had to do was to convince Kate to be his friend. His friend with benefits. Marital benefits, that was.

Chapter Eightteen

The days passed quickly for Kate, the nights not so much. Her kissing Jared had been a mistake because all she could think about was another kiss.

Ugh. She lay in her bed. Three o'clock in the morning, according to the digital clock on the nightstand. She should be fast asleep, not wide-awake, but thinking about him in the guest bedroom down the hall wasn't helping. She kept waiting for Cassidy—

The baby.

Kate bolted upright.

Cassidy hadn't woken up tonight.

That wasn't normal.

Heart pounding, Kate hurried to the baby's room. The door was ajar. She peeked inside.

Cassidy lay with her hands behind her head, sound asleep. Her tiny chest rose with her breaths. So small, so perfect.

Even when she fussed or cried.

As Kate's pulse returned to normal, love for the child welled inside of her. She'd finally found what had eluded her all these years—unconditional love. Kate hadn't believed it was possible for a person to love her no matter what she said or did.

But Cassidy did.

Thank you, Susan. Thank you so very much.

As Kate watched the baby sleep, she sensed a presence behind her—Jared. What would it take for him to love her the way the baby did? Without reserve. Without conditions. Totally. Completely.

Forever.

She backed out of the room and closed the door until only a slight crack remained.

He yawned. "I heard you get up."

Stubble covered his face. His tousled hair and sleep-rumpled T-shirt and boxer briefs made him look sexy—a tad dangerous.

Her pulse quickened.

Forget cardio exercise. Between Cassidy and Jared, Kate's heart received enough of a workout.

"Sorry," she said. "I was worried."

He took a step toward the baby's room. "Is something wrong, Kate?"

Her heart thudded. Jared adored Cassidy and had

jumped into his new role as a stay-at-home dad without regrets.

Kate respected that, respected him. "She didn't wake up tonight. I wanted to make sure she was okay."

He straightened. "And?"

"She's fine. Sound asleep. The way she should be."

"Good."

Kate forced herself to nod. She didn't trust her voice, not when she was thinking about how handsome he looked and how she was tired of waking up alone. But that was loneliness talking. And attraction. Two things that would only complicate matters.

"We may have turned a corner," he added.

A knot formed in her throat. "Corner?"

"Cassidy is sleeping through the night."

"That would be great."

Except then, he would be free to go home. If the baby adjusted to her nap schedule and no longer threw tantrums at bedtime, he had no reason to stay.

Her chest tightened. Kate didn't want him to leave. Which was why a part of her hoped tonight was an anomaly. She wasn't ready to say goodbye to him.

"You'd better get some sleep," Jared said. "Don't you have a big meeting tomorrow?"

She always had a big meeting, but she appreciated him remembering. If only he would sweep her off her feet and carry her to bed the way he used to. "I have one."

"I'll take care of Cassidy if she wakes up."

"Thanks." Kate trudged to her bedroom, making sure she didn't look back. If she saw him watching her, she wouldn't be able to close the door.

Kate stepped into her room, shut the door, and clicked the lock in place.

What was she going to do? Jared made her life so much better. The way he handled the house and the baby helped, but his lending a hand or an ear made such a difference. They ate dinner together, shared their days, and helped each other with the chores. They'd become partners, teammates, and parents. Kate didn't know how she would get along without him.

And that was a problem.

The problem.

They were playing house. She got that part.

But being "mom" when she was used to kissing and touching "dad" who walked around in a T-shirt and underwear looking better than a model wasn't fun. Or easy to do and ignore the undercurrents of attraction.

Especially when the lines between make-believe and real life kept blurring.

At least they did for her.

While having Jared here to help with Cassidy was wonderful, it wasn't enough for Kate.

It would never be enough.

But nothing she did could change that.

* * *

The following Thursday, Jared pushed Cassidy in her stroller along the waterfront path in downtown Portland. His sisters, Heather and Hannah, pushed strollers alongside him.

"How are things going?" Heather asked.

"Good," he said. "It's going well with Cassidy."

"Any change in your arrangement with Kate?" Hannah's suggestive lift of her eyebrows only added to the curiosity in her voice.

Not the change she meant. "Not as much as I hoped for."

"And what were you hoping for?" Heather asked. "That she would show up in your bed naked and attack you?"

He half laughed. "Pretty much."

His sisters shook their heads.

But it wasn't only about sex or the lack of it. Somewhere between caring for Cassidy and living together as a family, he and Kate had become a team, a parental unit, a couple. Their bond grew stronger every day. Jared didn't want to lose that when he returned to Seattle.

"She's my wife," he said. "It shouldn't be this difficult."

Hannah sighed. "You've never had a conventional marriage, little brother."

"And Kate filed for divorce," Heather said. "It won't be an easy road ahead."

"I'm not giving up," he said.

"Have you thought about what will happen if everything you're doing, all the sacrifices you're making, don't change things?" Heather asked.

"No." He glanced at a ship sailing on the Willamette River. "Losing isn't an option. I'll make my marriage work."

Jared would do whatever it took. He would not fail.

Kate would fall in love with him again.

It was just a matter of time.

Unfortunately, his boss had called and wanted him back. On Monday. That only gave him three more days to make it happen.

* * *

Friday morning, her alarm blared. Eyes closed, Kate pounded the top of her nightstand until she found the snooze button. She wanted to sleep. And then she remembered—her staff meeting.

Kate glanced at the time.

Oh, no. Late.

She must have hit *snooze* more than once. She threw aside the covers, scrambled off the bed, and ran to the bathroom. Turning on the shower, she noticed no towels on the rack.

Oh, no. She was supposed to fold the load in the dryer last night.

Kate hurried to the laundry room, dug a towel from the dryer, and was halfway up the stairs when she bumped into Jared coming down.

She sucked in a breath.

No man should look this attractive so early. He wore a pair of shorts. And nothing else.

She swallowed. Hard.

"Good morning," he said with a smile. "In a hurry?"

Was she? Kate couldn't see past his chest and his tight abs. Her dry throat could teach the Sahara desert a thing or two. "Uh-huh."

"What are you doing down here?"

The sweat on his skin gleamed. Her temperature inched up.

"Kate?"

She showed him the towel, trying to concentrate on the damp tendrils framing his face so her gaze wouldn't drift lower.

"I need one, too," he said.

"Dryer." The word burst from her lips. "The towels are in the dryer. I forgot to fold the laundry."

"I'll fold it."

His good looks, his rich voice, and his glistening skin wreaked havoc with her senses. She didn't like that. "It's my turn."

"I don't mind."

But she did. "I want to do...my share of chores."

No, what Kate wanted to do was kiss him.

Forget the rules. Forget friendly kisses. Bring on the hot ones.

She gulped.

His gaze raked over her, reminding her she was wearing only a T-shirt. And a short one at that. As her cheeks warmed, she tugged on the hemline.

"Don't do that." His voice sent a ripple of awareness through her. "Your curves are coming back. I like it."

And she liked him. A singsong rhyme from her school days played in her head. Kate and Jared sitting in a tree K-I-S-S-I-N-G. Forget the tree. The stairs would work fine.

She had to get a grip. Or take a spin on the dryer's cooldown cycle.

Remember the rules. Set boundaries. Keep her distance.

So what if he had a fantastic body? And looked gorgeous after finishing a rep of crunches or push-ups or whatever he did to stay fit. He was still just a guy. Man. Dad.

Who was leaving for Seattle on Sunday.

She clutched the towel.

Unless she wanted to hand him her heart with a Fragile Do Not Break sticker attached, she must stop ogling him like a new pair of shoes. "I need a shower."

"Me, too." The invitation in his eyes tightened her chest, and she struggled to breathe. "Want to join me?"

Yes. No. What if the baby woke up? "I'm running late."

"You can go first, Katie."

"Thanks." But he wasn't doing her any favors.

He walked past her, brushing his shoulder against her bare arm. Accidental or on purpose, she didn't know, but heat exploded at the point of contact. The attraction between them had grown.

Bad. Very bad.

"And, Kate," he called.

She glanced back.

"Make sure you leave me some hot water."

That wouldn't be a problem. The coldest setting was probably too warm for her.

"Don't worry," she said. "You'll have plenty."

* * *

She wanted him. Thanks to their early morning encounter on the stairs, Jared knew it. He'd won.

W-O-N.

Tonight, he would talk to Kate about making this marriage of convenience more convenient and real. He wanted his wife—body, heart, and soul.

His cell phone rang. He recognized his lawyer's name and number on the screen. "Hello."

But as his attorney updated him, Jared's hope and conviction died. His day had been great up to this point, but now...

He disconnected from the call in a state of shock that failed to block his rising anger. Or his hurt.

Jared had been wrong. Kate didn't want him. She never had.

He scooped a crying Cassidy from her crib and prepared her bottle with jerky efficiency.

When he heard Kate's car in the driveway a few minutes later, he stalked to the door to meet her.

"Hello," Kate said with a smile. She kissed the baby's cheek and then his. "How was your day?"

The shirt collar tightened around his neck. "My day was going fine until I got a phone call from my lawyer telling me the judge signed the judgment of dissolution of our marriage."

"Oh, no." The color drained from Kate's face. She covered her gaping mouth with her hands. "I'm so sorry. I never told my attorney to stop the divorce proceedings."

Her obvious shock reassured him. A little. "Did you forget—?"

"Of course I forgot." She glared at him. "Do you think I would do this on purpose?"

And chance losing Cassidy?

No. But the betrayal, intentional or not, cut deeply. Letting it go wasn't so easy. "Probably not."

"Definitely not." Kate might have changed and

softened some of her edges, but she still had a spine. She looked him squarely in the eyes. "Between the baby, work, and you being here, I've been busy. I agreed to the arrangement, and I'm sticking to that. No matter what."

The sincerity in her voice removed what doubt remained. Jared's anger dissipated. "I believe you."

Her gaze held his. The connection between them was still there, though dimmed by a fog of distrust and hurt.

"So what happens now?" she asked.

"There is a thirty-day waiting period until the dissolution is final," he explained, having memorized his lawyer's words. "If we want to stay together and give notice to the court, our marriage will continue as if we never filed for divorce."

She pulled out her cell phone. "Let's call now."

Her eagerness pleased Jared, but not even Kate's determination would turn back the clock. "It's after five. The courts are closed until Monday."

Anxiousness gleamed in her eyes. "You'll be in Seattle then."

Kate sounded so sad, looked so lost.

"It'll be okay." But Jared's words did nothing to remove the heaviness centered in his chest. "We're in this together, remember?"

But suddenly that didn't seem nearly enough.

Chapter Nineteen

"I can't believe it's time for me to go home," Jared said as he opened his suitcase. Especially when he'd wanted to return with his family in tow.

Sitting crisscross on the guest room floor, Kate folded his clothes. "The time's gone so fast."

He was glad she agreed. "I want to pack the entire house and bring it with me to Seattle."

"Do you have that much space in your apartment?"

"I'll make it fit. Anything for us to be together."

"We'll see each other on weekends."

"Is that enough for you?"

She stuck out her chin. "It has to be."

"Does it?" he pressed, knowing tomorrow he didn't want to say goodbye to her for one day, let alone five.

"Yes, it does." She looked away. "Please don't make this any harder than it has to be."

The emotion in her voice gave him hope. "I don't want this to be hard. I just want us to be together."

"Me, too." She folded a T-shirt with the same competence she did everything else and handed the neat, white square to him. "Leave some clothes here so you won't have to pack an extra bag when you come down on weekends."

"You're so practical, Kate." He'd always respected that trait, but her practicality was getting in the way of what he wanted—what he knew was best for her, him, and Cassidy. Jared placed the T-shirt on top of his shorts.

"I have to be to take care of the baby."

"It won't be easy for you." That bothered him. Regular meals had helped her put on weight. A full night's sleep had gotten rid of the dark circles under her eyes. She appeared healthier and rested. He didn't want her to fall back into the old routine of neglecting herself when things got hectic. "I hate leaving you."

"I hate to see you go." She smiled ruefully. "It's been great having you here. I'll admit I have no idea how I'll get along without you."

"Come with me."

"To Seattle?"

"Yes."

For a second, the idea took hold in her eyes, and then her familiar caution and practicality returned.

"You mean, next weekend?"

"For good." He tossed a pair of pants in his suitcase, not caring if they were folded. "I don't want to be apart."

"I'd love it if we were together, but this isn't only about us."

"The two of us together would be best for Cassidy."

"I meant my firm," Kate corrected, her voice strong and determined. "Twenty people rely on me for their livelihood. The potential for growth is phenomenal. It makes financial sense for me to guide the company through this period and ensure our family's future."

Financial sense, sure. But with a suitcase half-packed and facing a week of late-night calls from a hotel room in Boston while he met with a client, he didn't want to be sensible. He'd keep the no-sex rule in place if it meant having her with him.

"Have Emily Butler run the firm for a while," he said. "She seems sharp with a lot of savvy."

"She is, and a dedicated worker, too. But she's pregnant and taking maternity leave this summer."

"There has to be someone else."

"It's my company. My name's on the placard."

"You're my wife and Cassidy's mother."

"That's not fair." Kate frowned. "I shouldn't have to choose. Why do I have to be the one who has to give up my career?"

"Because that's how life works sometimes. Cassidy needs her mother."

Kate rolled her eyes. "Your father would say that it's a woman's place to sacrifice. But I won't do it."

Brady and Susan popped into Jared's mind. "Life isn't always fair."

"I want to be your wife and Cassidy's mom, but you're asking me to give up"—Kate took a breath and exhaled slowly—"my home, my career, my life. Everything I've worked for and dreamed of since I was young. I can't put myself in a position of having nothing, of being destitute when you leave me for good."

"What do you mean? I'm not leaving you. I want us to be together." He sympathized with her, but too much was riding on this to let it go. Weren't his dreams as important as hers? Wasn't their family? He needed to play to win. Even if it was dirty. The means justified the ends, as his father always said. "Isn't having a family part of your dream?"

"You know it is."

"So how can you walk away from one? From us?"

"I'm not walking away." She crossed her arms over her chest. "I don't want to fight."

"We need to discuss this."

"The last time we discussed this, we ended up in divorce court." Her eyes pleaded with him. "It's too soon for me to make the decision you want."

"It's been two weeks."

"Two wonderful weeks. And that's part of the problem. We shouldn't decide when our judgment is clouded."

"I've made up my mind. I want you, Kate. I want you and Cassidy in my life."

"We are in your life."

"But not where I want you." He took her hands in his. "We could have a real marriage if you moved to Seattle with me."

"We could still have one if I didn't."

"Is that what you want?" he asked, tension charging the air. "Because I'd be willing to work with that."

* * *

Kate spent a restless night in her big, empty bed with Jared on her mind. She missed him so much. And he wasn't even gone yet. His words kept echoing through her head.

I'd be willing to work with that.

She was tempted if it meant not having to give up her company and her home to be with him. The marriage of convenience was getting harder with her attraction for him growing each day. Maybe they could try and see what happened. Though if it imploded, that might ruin everything.

"Happy Mother's Day."

Great. Jared was leaving tonight, and all she

wanted to do was dream about him, complete with realistic audio. She needed to gain control over her emotions.

The mattress depressed.

She opened her eyes.

Jared sat next to her with Cassidy in his arms. He'd ditched his T-shirt and shorts for a black polo shirt and khaki slacks. The smart-casual look suited him well, as did the way his damp hair curled at the ends. She fought the urge to reach out and touch him.

He looked good, so mouthwatering good.

Kate wondered if she was still dreaming. She propped herself up on her elbows. Nope. She was awake. "About last night."

As he smiled, his dimples appeared with a vengeance, leaving her sucker punched. "Not now."

But they hadn't come to any conclusion, decision. And Jared would return to Seattle. Tonight.

He watched her with an odd expression in his eyes and motioned toward the other side of the bed. A pink smoothie, a chocolate doughnut, a white envelope, a blue box, and a single red rose were on a tray.

Wow. Kate sat up. "What's going on?"

"It's for you."

Presents. After they'd fought. That made no sense. Confused, she looked at him. "I don't understand."

"Happy Mother's Day," he said.

Cassidy giggled and waved her hands.

Mother's Day. Kate was now a mother.

A swell of emotion swept through her. Tears stung her eyes. She hadn't expected this. Today had been nothing but when Jared returned to Seattle.

"Did you think I would forget?" he asked.

Not trusting her voice, she shook her head. "I forgot."

"You've been busy."

"It's not that," she admitted, overwhelmed by and unworthy of the attention. "I spent so many years celebrating this day with different mothers but never my own. I know the holiday is a big deal for your family, but it never seemed important to me."

"Today is the start of a new tradition, then."

Their first one.

Cassidy grinned.

Kate wiped the drool from the baby's chin with the sleeve of her nightshirt.

"Koo," the baby said.

A sudden squeezing pain sliced through her. "This should be Susan's day."

"Susan would be proud of you. She would appreciate everything you're doing for her daughter." Jared traced Kate's jawline with his fingertip. "The way I do."

"Thank you so much." Kate sniffled. "You don't know what this means to me."

She kissed Cassidy's cheek. She went to kiss

Jared's, but he turned, so she kissed him on the lips, instead. He tasted warm and sweet, a mix of coffee and chocolate doughnuts.

Jared grinned. "Gotcha."

He did. He had her. All of her.

The realization left her speechless and scared. She didn't want Jared to leave tonight, but she couldn't go with him, either. But he was willing to try it another way.

Was that enough?

He reached over her and picked up a rectangular navy-blue box patterned like the stripes on a grosgrain ribbon. "This is for you."

She untied the blue and white ribbon imprinted with the name Aaron Basha and removed the lid. Inside lay a silver—no, white gold—charm bracelet and the prettiest pink enamel baby shoe charm with a diamond strap and diamond hearts on the toe. "I love it."

"Let me put the bracelet on you." He laid the baby on the bed and clasped the chain around her wrist.

"This was so thoughtful of you." She stared at the dangling charm. "Thank you."

He handed her the white envelope. "Now, this."

Kate pulled out a lovely card with a little girl walking through a field of purple irises and green grass. The printed sentiment brought a lump to her throat, but the handwritten words at the bottom made her heart skip a beat. Okay, three. She reread them.

Katie,

You are my wife and my life. Whether I'm here or in Seattle, that won't change. Forget the rules. I want a real marriage with you. I want us to be a real family. All you have to do is say the word.

Love,
Jared (& Cassidy, too!)

Kate stared into his eyes. Her brain shouted a warning, but her heart didn't want to listen. Even though she knew the risks, she wanted to take the chance. She wanted the same things Jared did.

A real marriage and a real family.

That was the bottom line.

Cassidy deserved parents who loved each other, not ones who were together in name only.

Long-distance wouldn't be easy, but if they communicated and each made an effort, they would make it work.

She cleared her throat. "Yes."

A nerve twitched at his neck. "Yes?"

"Isn't that the word I'm supposed to say to make things...real?"

A smile erupted on his face, not only with dimples but lines crinkling the corner of his eyes. He gathered her up in his arm.

The tender affection in his gaze sent her heart soaring with happiness.

He lowered his mouth to hers.

The moment his lips touched hers, emotion burst through Kate with the force of a rocket launcher. She could no longer pretend she felt nothing and hold back her feelings for Jared.

He pressed his lips against hers. The warmth filled her up. This closeness was what she'd been missing, what she needed. And Kate never wanted the kiss to end.

Heat emanated deep within her, but Cassidy was here with them. Maybe that was why Jared held back, not touching her, as if he were conscious of the baby's presence, too.

They were a family, and sometimes that meant having to wait even if you didn't want to.

"Ah-gah, gah."

Jared slowly drew the kiss to an end. "Cassidy is getting bored."

That was the least boring kiss ever. Kate's mouth felt bruised and utterly loved. She inhaled to calm her rapid pulse and fill her lungs with much-needed air. "Um, Jared, that wasn't a friendly kiss."

Mischief gleamed in his eyes. "Now that we're husband and wife for real and not in name only, the marital kiss takes precedence over the friend kiss."

"I can live with that."

"Then it's official."

Cassidy squealed with delight.

"Group hug." Jared picked up the baby. "Or should I say, family hug."

"We're a family, Cassidy," Kate said. "A real family."

He smiled. "I like the sound of that."

"You know what I'd like right now?"

"Me, too." He glanced at the clock. "But it's too early to put Cassidy down for her nap."

"I hate to pop your bubble, but this"—Kate patted the mattress—"isn't what I was talking about?"

Lines creased his forehead. "What do you want?"

"Breakfast." She grinned mischievously. "That doughnut smells yummy."

"I'm supposed to be the yummy one." As he sighed, he stared at Cassidy. "Your mommy has the wrong thing on her mind this morning."

"No, she's just more practical about our other commitments, like meeting your family at church in an hour."

Jared groaned. "You're no fun."

"Wait until we get home," she promised. "I'll show you how fun I can be."

He raised a brow. "What do you have in mind?"

"One last present for Mother's Day."

"What?"

She met his gaze directly. "You."

He sucked in a breath. "Should I wear a bow?"

"Please do," she said in her huskiest voice.

"Anything else?"

Kate winked. "That's up to you."

Chapter Twenty

A few hours later, Jared stared at Kate, who sat with Cassidy in his parents' backyard. It was a perfect day to celebrate. The sun shone brightly in the sky. The laughter of his nieces and nephews filled the air. But he couldn't wait to be alone with his wife.

His father flipped the steaks and hamburgers cooking on the grill. "That baby gets cuter each time I see her."

Every Mother's Day under the shady canopy of the towering Douglas firs and the blossoming cherry trees, his dad threw a barbecue for his wife, daughters, and daughters-in-law. One of the many family traditions Jared had grown up with, but this year held more importance to him because of Cassidy and what today meant for Kate.

"Kate looks good," his father added. "Not so skinny and pale."

Jared nodded. She looked radiant, her face glowing.

"So, you're heading back to Seattle tonight?" his dad asked.

"Yes." But Jared wasn't thinking that far ahead. He only wanted to get home. Speaking of which, he needed to swipe a bow from the pile of presents on the picnic table. "I'll be back on Friday."

Sooner, if he got the opportunity.

His father studied him. "Is this long-distance arrangement going to last?"

"Yes." Jared hated rehashing the details with each member of his family as if they knew more about the situation than he did. "Kate and I will make our marriage work."

"Your mother mentioned the judge signing the official dissolution."

"Seems like Mom told everybody." He took a sip of his iced tea. "We're taking care of that tomorrow."

His dad peppered the meat. "Or you could use this to your advantage."

Jared swallowed a groan. "I don't—"

"Hear me out, son."

Even though he knew what was coming, he nodded.

"Threaten to follow through with the divorce to force Kate to move to Seattle," his dad suggested.

"You know she'd do anything not to lose Cassidy."

Bitterness coated Jared's mouth. "Funny, but you're not the first person to tell me that today."

His brothers and sisters had mentioned a similar idea. Which meant their dad was the ringleader. Heat flowed through Jared.

His father adjusted the temperature on the gas grill. "So? It would get your family in Seattle that much sooner. That's what matters."

Jared's muscles bunched. "I can't do that to my wife, Dad."

"Can't or won't? Sometimes a man has to do things he'd rather not, but the means justify the end, son. Kate will thank you for this later."

Except she hadn't the first time around. Jared had lost Kate by leaving without her. And if he did this...

A stunt like that would be unforgivable. He would lose any hope of a reconciliation. And rightly so. "No."

"You've worked too hard for your career." His dad put hot dogs onto a serving platter. "You can easily support a family on your income. Once Cassidy is older, Kate can go back to work at a PR firm up there. She doesn't need to run a company. That would be too difficult with a child and your travel schedule."

As the words sank in, unease slithered through Jared. He'd had similar thoughts, which was why the move to Seattle made more sense to him than staying in Portland. And that meant...

Kate was one hundred percent correct.

He *was* turning into his father. He'd been selfish, putting himself first and seeing them in the traditional role models of his parents. No wonder Kate bailed on him and their marriage.

Frank Reed was a good man, and Jared loved him, but following his dad's advice would be catastrophic and destroy everything.

Jared wanted—needed—to be a different kind of husband. Kate's partner in every sense of the word. That meant making decisions together and compromising, even sacrificing. But it all shouldn't be on her. She'd tried to tell him, but he hadn't heard her. Instead, he'd listened to his family. He wouldn't make the same mistake again. No way would he play games with his wife, forcing her to do what he wanted by threatening divorce and taking custody of Cassidy.

He stared across the grass at Kate, who helped the baby toss a ball in the air. "She'd hate me. And she'd have every right."

"You've been watching too many daytime talk shows these past two weeks." His dad laughed. "You're going soft."

Not soft. Just a bit more evolved. Jared shook his empty glass. "I need a refill."

"Consider what I said."

"I don't have to. I won't do that to her. To us."

"Somebody has to do something."

As Jared headed into the kitchen, he hoped his

father cooled down, so they could enjoy a pleasant lunch.

After they ate, his mother and sisters cleared away the dirty dishes. Jared picked up the wrapping paper from the gifts.

His dad approached Kate. "You ought to go with him."

She held the baby tighter. "I'm sorry, Frank. This arrangement is better for us."

"It's not good for Jared."

Jared dropped the paper and hurried over to them. "Dad, that's enough."

"The judge signed the paperwork," his father continued. "Jared has every right to follow through with the divorce if you won't go with him to Seattle."

Kate drew in a breath, her stricken eyes seeking Jared's. "Would you do that?"

"No." Jared had never understood her concerns about his family's intrusiveness, but he did now. It was time to stop it. "We've put up with the nosiness and your advice, but today a few of you went too far, suggesting what Dad just told Kate I should do, and that's wrong."

"You all should be ashamed of yourselves." Margery rushed to Kate's side like a mama bear protecting her cub. "I apologize for my misguided children. Especially the old one who should know better."

A red-faced Frank mumbled an apology.

"We wanted to help," Sam said.

Hannah nodded. So did Tucker. And Heather.

Jared listened to his family justify their reasons to him, but they were completely missing the point—missing who they should talk to. It wasn't him.

Disappointment weighed him down, but he saw things clearer. He'd always considered family, family. Extended, immediate, distant. It hadn't mattered.

Until today.

He loved his parents, brothers, and sisters, but he had his own family now, and they needed to come first.

"I'm not the one you should apologize to." Jared stared at his father and four siblings. "I know you want to help. That's what we do for each other. Help. Because we love each other so much. But you all need to think about what you asked me to do. There's no justification for this. The end doesn't justify the means, especially if it hurts the one person who matters the most to me. My wife."

Contrite expressions were on his dad's, sisters', and brothers' faces. But that wasn't enough.

"I'm the idiot who followed the advice and moved to Seattle without his wife. That was my choice, so stop blaming Kate and laying everything on her. Until you do that, we won't be back." Jared hated making a scene, but his family had left him no choice. He put his arm around her and the baby. "Let's go home."

* * *

In the car, Kate dabbed tears from the corners of her eyes. She'd respected and loved Jared before, but those feelings for him didn't compare to the ones now.

She was used to handling everything and making a place for herself. She'd done those things to avoid being disappointed. It was easier that way—safer. But today, Jared had taken on his father and siblings for her.

With no prompting.

Without being asked.

Her astonished heart overflowed with joy. "I can't believe what you said to your family."

"I'm sorry it had to come to that." Regret sounded in his voice, but the sincerity filled her with warmth.

She was no longer alone. "I'm not."

He glanced her way. "You're not?"

"Nope." Kate wouldn't take his championing her for granted. "No one has ever stood up for me like that. You made me feel good. Special. Thank you."

"I only did what needed to be done." Jared covered her hand with his. "I should have spoken up earlier, but I didn't realize..."

Staring at their linked fingers, at the pink baby shoe charm on the new bracelet around her wrist, everything she needed dangled at her fingertips. She wanted to reach out and grasp all of it. All she had to do was prove herself deserving of him the way he'd proved himself deserving of her.

Kate could make their marriage work. She loved him. No doubt. She wanted to be with him. No question.

Jared's actions today showed her he hadn't abandoned her by moving to Seattle without her. Instead of dealing with the troubles in their marriage, he'd listened to his family. He hadn't done that today.

He'd defended her.

He'd changed.

She felt renewed, alive, loved. She didn't want that to end. "So, what you said about moving to Seattle..."

He squeezed her hand. "I won't force you to move."

Kate drew strength from his touch. Love flowed from him, and it was her turn to let him experience it. "But that's what you want."

"I want us to be together."

"I want that, too."

Before she'd tried to control Jared because she'd had so little control of her own life. But they were a couple, a family, and her operating the same way would be destructive. Family sacrificed for each other. If she wanted to keep their family together, to make their marriage work, Kate would have to prove herself worthy of his love.

She took a deep breath. "What if Cassidy and I move to Seattle, and I try telecommuting? I'd probably have to set up a satellite office and travel some."

Jared pulled into the driveway and turned off the car. "You would do that?"

"I'm willing to see if it works," she said. "If it does, we can talk about what the next step would be."

Like the house. Her firm. So many things. "I need to find child care. I can't work while taking care of Cassidy at the same time."

"No problem. We can hire a nanny or use daycare." He sounded happy, but his gaze narrowed. "Are you sure about this, Katie?"

She had the family she'd dreamed about. A husband who'd stood up to his family in her defense and drawn a line with them. A daughter who loved her no matter what. Kate wouldn't risk that. She would do whatever having a real marriage and keeping her family together took. That meant being the perfect wife, mother, and businesswoman, too. She could do it. She would do it. "Yes, I'm sure."

Jared opened his door. "Stay here."

"Why?"

He removed a sleeping Cassidy from her car seat and grabbed the diaper bag. "Give me five minutes. That's all I ask."

"Okay." Kate would use the time to plan how a move to Seattle would work...

Four minutes later, a text message appeared on her cell phone: *Go upstairs.*

Kate did. All the doors were closed except the one to her bedroom. She stepped inside. "Jared?"

"Are you ready?" he called from the bathroom.

"For what?"

He walked out wearing a red bow. "To unwrap your present."

Chapter Twenty-One

J ared had won. He'd gotten what he wanted. Kate had called her attorney and stopped the divorce. She and Cassidy had been living in his apartment for the past two weeks.

So how come his victory felt so hollow?

He stared out the window of his hotel room on San Francisco's Union Square. His meeting with a CEO had gone well. Tomorrow he would tour the manufacturing facilities; the next day he would attend more meetings, and after that...

He hoped to finish in the morning and catch an earlier flight home.

Home.

Jared had only been home for five days since Kate and Cassidy arrived in Seattle. Unfortunately, the move hadn't solved the problem of their spending more time together. Granted, he would see them less if he added in a weekly commute to Portland, but was that worth disrupting their lives?

He'd tried to think of a solution, but work required constant travel, often weeks away at a time, visiting companies his clients wanted to invest in. What could he do? He loved his job, except...

He had more in his life to go home to now.

Jared stepped from the window and sat on the bed. Numbers needed to be crunched and research completed, but he didn't open his laptop. Instead, he grabbed his cell phone and hit the number three on his keypad.

On the fourth ring, a "hello" sounded that was sweeter than the song of a heavenly choir. Okay, he was exaggerating, but only slightly.

"Hey, gorgeous," he said.

"Jared? Hang on a minute."

As silence filled the receiver, he ignored the twinge of disappointment. He wanted to talk to Kate, not wait and wonder what she was doing without him.

"I'm back," she said less than thirty seconds later.

"You sound surprised to hear from me. Who else would call you at this hour?"

"I don't know," she teased. "Maybe a tall, dark, and handsome stranger."

"Well, I'm not a stranger." Though he worried about all the time he spent on the road, that Cassidy would forget who he was.

"You're not modest, either." Kate sounded like she was smiling.

"So, how are my two girls?"

"Cassidy's been a little fussy. Her first tooth came in."

"Yeah?" He sank into a king-size down pillow. "Sorry I missed that."

"There will be other teeth," Kate said as if trying to reassure him.

It didn't work.

"Others aren't the same as the first one." Jared wondered what milestones he might miss. Cassidy's first step, her first word, her first boyfriend.

"I'll e-mail you a picture."

His dissatisfaction grew. "I don't want to watch Cassidy grow up on a computer screen."

Silence.

"I'll text the pictures." Her lightness sounded forced.

"Are you getting any sleep?" he asked, instantly concerned and wanting to see her face.

"Cassidy's sticking to her schedule," Kate said, not answering his question.

He'd try a different tactic. "How's work?"

"It's heating up a bit."

"Trouble?"

"beBuzz has turned into a bigger project than we expected."

Her strained voice bothered him. "Are you okay?"

"A little tired." As she spoke, something muffled sounded in the background. "How about you? Are you okay?"

"I'll be better when I'm home." He'd memorized his itinerary. "Only three more days."

More silence greeted him.

"Kate?"

"Sorry," she said absently. "I thought I heard the baby."

She sounded distracted. Was she worried about Cassidy? He should let her go. "I'm going to do some work before bed."

"Me, too. Good—"

"Wait." Jared wasn't ready to say goodbye. "I miss you, Kate. I really miss you and Cassidy."

"I miss you, too. A lot."

"I'll call tomorrow." He hated to hang up, but the longer he stayed on, the later she would have to stay up to finish her work. Despite her denial that Cassidy had gotten off her schedule, Kate sounded tired. "Bye."

He disconnected the line. The call didn't fill the void inside him. He sat in lonely silence, thinking about her voice and her words.

I miss you, too. A lot.

She wanted him home; he wanted to be there.

Three more days. Less than seventy-two hours until he saw her again. Jared could make it. He had no other choice.

214

* * *

Kate stared at the receiver in her hand. Her heart ached. She missed Jared more than she thought possible. If only he were here...

But he wasn't and wouldn't be. She might have moved to Seattle, but he was gone all the time. She'd known that would be the case. *Still*... She sighed.

At least she saw Cassidy's new tooth.

Kate returned to the compact apartment kitchen that was now the satellite office for her public relations firm. Two employees worked at the table covered with laptops, paper, and a speakerphone. Next to them on the floor, Cassidy sat in her lilac baby seat.

Kate smiled at her. "That was your daddy. He misses us."

Us.

The word warmed her heart. That counted for something.

Sean Owens, her assistant and the crush of the unmarried females in the office, adjusted his black-rimmed glasses. "Is Jared coming home?"

"He'll be back as soon as he can." Kate didn't like her employees knowing about her personal life, but in this case, she'd had no choice. "Friday at the latest."

Maisie McFall, a thirty-something writer with short, spiky black hair, and four years of nanny experience, looked up from her laptop. "If you were in Portland, this situation would be easier to manage."

Her words echoed Kate's doubts. If she were in Portland, her life would be easier and back to normal, too. She stared at the charm bracelet around her wrist.

"I told Jared I'd give Seattle a try." He'd proven his love. It was her turn. "I have to do that."

And she would. She had to.

Kate understood what was at stake. She needed to make sure they remained together because she was the only one who knew what the lack of a family could do, not just to her and Jared, but to Cassidy. Kate had spent her entire childhood trying and failing to fit in, to be a part of other people's families. She wouldn't fail with her own family.

Sean refilled her coffee cup. "If this situation with beBuzz gets any worse..."

Her newest client was facing an onslaught of bad press. Accusations of misrepresenting their latest financial report had resulted in the "resignation" of the CEO and CFO, and a downward spiral of the highly touted stock. If the negative publicity and hints of criminal activity continued, the once-thriving company would face bankruptcy—or worse.

"I know what's at stake." Not only for her client, but also for her firm. "I appreciate you coming up here today. Between you and the team in the office, we'll get this done."

Another all-nighter, no doubt. The second in a row for her, but she hadn't told Jared. Why worry him when he was so far away?

Cassidy yawned.

"I'm putting the baby to bed. I'll be right back." As Kate picked up the baby, Cassidy puckered. "Don't get that look on your face. It's bedtime. Be a good girl and go to sleep."

Cassidy pouted, her lower lip quivering.

Kate kissed the baby's cheek. Hot. "Oh, no."

"What is it?" Maisie asked, already on her feet.

"Cassidy's burning up." Kate touched the baby's forehead. "I'm sure she has a fever."

* * *

"Have you run over the schedule for the new CEO's interview on CNBC?" Kate asked during a conference call two days later. She held Cassidy. Antibiotics helped the baby's ear infection, but she was off-schedule, and so was Kate. If not for caffeine, she would be flat on her back comatose.

You're the incredible one, Kate. I'm amazed at how much you've done with Cassidy. You can handle anything.

Kate hadn't told Jared about the ear infection, about the problems with beBuzz, or pulling all-nighters. He believed she could handle anything. And she didn't want to disappoint him. Not that it would matter to him anyway.

Okay, that was tiredness talking. But Kate wasn't sure how much more she could take.

On the other end of the speakerphone, someone

droned on. She massaged an aching temple.

Sean hit *Mute*. "This isn't looking good."

"Have faith." That was all they had left.

Cassidy whimpered.

Frustrated, Kate sighed. She should take her own advice and have faith herself. "Are you hungry, baby?"

"I'll take her." Maisie stood. "Cassidy and I have an understanding with eating. The messier, the better. Isn't that right, baby?"

"Thanks." Guilt mixed with gratitude. Kate owed both employees for going above and beyond with beBuzz and Cassidy. Jared would be back tomorrow, and by then, Kate hoped things settled down both on the home and work fronts.

"Look at this, Kate," Sean said.

As Maisie strapped the baby into the high chair, Kate sat at the table and stared at the chart on Sean's laptop. beBuzz's stock was up eight percent since the market opened two hours ago. A good sign after a fifty-seven percent drop this week. "The damage control is working."

Sean nodded. "You're the spin master."

Kate wouldn't disagree. The room *was* sort of spinning. As she rubbed her forehead, she glanced at the baby eating her rice cereal. White mush seemed to be everywhere but inside Cassidy's mouth.

"We're not out of the woods yet." Maisie wiped the baby's face with a...dish towel.

Were they out of washcloths and napkins?

"Okay," Emily Butler, second-in-command at the Portland office, said finally. "We have the schedule, and I will accompany Mr. Leclerc to the studio for his interview and the press conference."

Kate hit the speaker button. "Sounds good. The stock is up slightly, but we have a long way to go. We need an all-out blitz today."

As she stood, the chart on the screen blurred. Kate blinked and refocused. Lack of sleep was catching up with her. She headed to the overused but well-appreciated coffeepot.

Reaching for a cup in the upper cabinet, she felt woozy. Shaky. Something crashed on the counter.

"Kate?" a voice asked from behind her.

Her legs wobbled. She reached for the counter.

I'm sorry, Jared. I failed you.

And then she saw...

Black.

Chapter Twenty-Two

Jared entered the hospital with only Kate on his mind. He hadn't been able to stop worrying about her since he received the call five excruciating hours ago. An older woman with blue-gray hair and a pink smock directed him to a waiting area where he found Sean, a coworker named Maisie, and Cassidy, in her stroller fast asleep.

The baby's happy expression brought momentary relief. At least she was fine.

"Where's Kate?" Jared asked. "How is she doing?"

"She's with the doctor," Sean explained. "Kate has a concussion. She hit her head when she collapsed."

"How did that happen?" Jared noticed the exchange of glances between his wife's employees.

"Talk to Kate about that," Sean said.

Jared wanted to do just that. "Would you mind watching Cassidy again?"

"I don't mind at all, Mr. Malone," Maisie said, and Jared saw no reason to correct her. "She's a great baby and takes her medicine from us without fussing much."

"Medicine?" Kate had mentioned nothing about the baby needing medication. "For what? Her new tooth?"

"An ear infection," Sean replied.

Jared's unease grew. His wife's employees knew more about his daughter than he did. "I'll be in Kate's room if you need me."

As he headed down the hospital corridor, memories of Boise plowed into him—running into Kate at Don's office, seeing Cassidy for the first time, saying goodbye to their best friends. But focusing on the past wouldn't help Kate. She needed him to be with her now.

Jared entered her room. She lay in the bed, an IV in her left arm, a white bandage on her forehead. Her pale face brought a rush of guilt.

Would this have happened if he hadn't been away?

A wave of nausea overtook his stomach.

The doctor, a young woman with thick black hair, cleared her throat.

As he forced a smile, Jared put on his game face.

"Hey."

"Hi," Kate mumbled, looking dazed. "Cassidy?"

"She's fine. Napping." He touched Kate's right hand. She seemed so fragile. "Sean and Maisie are with her in the waiting area. My parents are on the way."

"Okay. Good." Her voice faded.

The doctor greeted him. "I'm Dr. Pradhan."

"Jared Reed."

"Your wife has suffered a level-three concussion," Dr. Pradhan said. "The CT scan showed no skull fracture or bleeding, but we're keeping her overnight for observation."

"Is it serious?"

"Head injuries, especially with loss of consciousness, are always taken seriously, but a concussion is a type of closed head trauma and generally not considered a life-threatening injury. However, there can be short-term and long-term effects."

Not life-threatening.

Key point.

"I'm concerned about the level of fatigue that caused Kate's collapse in the first place," the doctor said.

"She fell because she was tired?"

Dr. Pradhan checked the chart. "Fainted would be a more accurate term based on the description of what happened."

Jared had wondered whether Kate would take care of herself when he wasn't around, but he never imagined she would wind up hospitalized. He didn't understand. She told him she was a little tired, but so was every working mom. She never hinted something was wrong or the baby ill. He scratched his head.

"Cassidy?" Kate asked.

She'd asked the same question before. That wasn't good. Worried, Jared looked at the doctor.

"Repeating the same thing over again is called perseverating and a symptom of a concussion," Dr. Pradhan explained. "Just answer Kate's question."

"Cassidy's fine." He patted her hand and stared at the charm bracelet around Kate's wrist. "She's in the waiting room with Sean and Maisie."

"Okay," Kate said.

Not okay. Jared hated this. He hated seeing her this way. He hated feeling as if he were somewhat to blame. He wanted to know what had happened.

"So what do we do, Doctor?" he asked.

"We wait."

* * *

Kate hurt. Her brain was mushy like leftover oatmeal. Either that, or someone had stuffed soggy cotton balls into her head. She opened her eyes. The light made her squint.

Hospital.

She was in the hospital.

And Cassidy...was okay.

Her pounding head and blurry vision made her squeeze her eyes shut. She opened them again and blinked. Jared came into focus, his intense gaze resting squarely on her.

He'd come back.

Her heart thumped. "You're here."

His soft smile practically caressed. "Where else would I be?"

"I—I missed you," she croaked. "Water, please."

As he pushed a button, her bed rose, so she was sitting up. Kate felt wobbly. As she adjusted to being upright, Jared poured her a glass.

She smelled flowers. Over Jared's shoulder, Kate saw bouquets of all shapes and sizes. She also noticed a box of her favorite chocolates.

He handed her the water. She drank. The liquid quenched her thirst and cleared a few of the dust bunnies from her mind. Enough so she remembered.

Reality crashed down on her. Everything she'd done, the perfect image she'd projected for so many years, had collapsed with her.

Over. It was all over.

Air whooshed from her lungs.

She nearly dropped her cup.

Jared took it from her before sitting on the edge of the bed, his thigh pressing against her. "Do you need anything?"

You.

The compassion on his face twisted her insides. Fear and uncertainty rooted themselves in her.

"Where is Cassidy?" Kate asked.

"With my parents," he said. "My entire family is here. They feel horrible for what happened on Mother's Day, and as soon as they heard you were in the hospital, they dropped everything and drove to Seattle. The baby is getting lots of attention."

The throbbing pain in Kate's head was nothing compared to the ache of her heart. She swallowed a sob. "I'm sorry. If I'd been holding Cassidy when I fainted..."

"But you weren't holding her." His warm, calm voice kept Kate afloat. "She's fine, and you'll be fine."

She wanted to believe him.

Since Cassidy had entered their lives, Jared had given her no reason to doubt him. Kate clung to that. She wanted him to hold her and tell her it was okay. That no matter what, he would love her and never leave her.

"I don't understand how this happened." Jared's hand covered hers. Warm and strong and protective. "We talked every day. You mentioned being tired, but you never told me about Cassidy's ear infection or a big crisis at work. Why didn't you tell me what was happening, Katie?"

Guilt coated her throat. Jared had been a good husband and a wonderful dad. He deserved an answer, but past hurts gripped hold of her. If she told him the truth, he would realize she couldn't do it all, that she wasn't perfect. That she had…failed.

Kate hoped the truth wouldn't matter. He'd proven he cared about her. He'd wanted to save their marriage. But what if Jared was like the other people in her life? People who didn't want her, who didn't love her, who abandoned her?

Did she trust him enough not to leave her?

Because if Jared left, he would take Cassidy with him.

An iron vise clamped around Kate's heart and squeezed hard, but the thought of losing the two people she loved most in the world would be nothing like the real thing.

Fear scraped her bare. Trust him or not; that was the question. She pressed her lips together.

As she pulled her hand from his, he tightened his grasp.

"Please, Kate."

His anguished tone cut into her like a knife. A wound would heal, but this...

She glanced around the room at everything except him. If she avoided his eyes, maybe she didn't have to answer him.

"Talk to me," he pressed.

Kate wanted to believe in him, but the possible consequences frightened her. If she told him, she could destroy the family they'd built together.

She stole a glance at Jared, expecting to see accusation and anger, but she saw only concern.

For her.

Emotion clogged her throat.

A muscle flicked at his jaw. As he closed his hand around hers, his forehead creased with worry. "If you can't trust me enough to talk to me..." His voice cracked. "We'll never make it."

Chapter Twenty-Three

Jared's words brought tears to Kate's eyes. She teetered between self-protection and full disclosure. Both had their risks, consequences that might change her life forever. But if she refused to tell him the truth, if she wouldn't trust him with that same truth, what did that say about their marriage? Their future? She entwined her fingers with his.

Logically she understood what to do, but her heart remained unconvinced. Not after years of having to prove herself worthy of a home, a family, love.

Kate gnawed on her bottom lip.

He scooted closer. "I want to make this work, but you have to meet me halfway."

"I let you down." As the words tumbled from her

mouth, she wanted to walk out on him before he did that to her. Her heart, however... Her heart wouldn't allow her to do that. "The day you left for San Francisco, we found ourselves in the middle of a media circus because of discrepancies in beBuzz's latest financial report."

"You never said a word about this."

"I thought...I believed I could handle it. Sean and Maisie came up to help. But Cassidy got sick, and I didn't have as much free time during the day, so I worked at night. All night."

Jared's brows knotted. "You just had to call me."

"And say what?" Frustration and fear burned in Kate's throat. "Fly home. I need to be in Portland because my company is falling apart without me?"

"Yes." His voice was firm. Positive. "I will drop everything if you need me. If you'd told me..."

"You have a responsibility to your boss and your clients."

"I have a responsibility to you. You're my wife. I had no idea anything was wrong until I got the call you were in the hospital. I couldn't think straight. I only wanted to get to you. As soon as possible."

"I didn't plan on this happening. I never wanted you to..."

"To what?"

She swallowed. "To know."

"Why?"

"Because I agreed to move to Seattle." Kate

struggled to keep her voice steady. "How could I make our marriage work and have us be a family if I kept running to Portland whenever something came up at the office?"

"But you said this was a crisis." Jared's jaw tensed.

The silence increased the tension in the air. Even though he sat next to her, the distance between them grew.

He blew out a breath. "If you would have told me how important—"

"I was afraid to tell you."

"Afraid of what?"

You can handle anything.

Kate forced herself to look at Jared. She would either destroy her marriage with the truth or save it. "Of disappointing you. I didn't want to lose you."

"You would never lose me."

"Yes, I would. If you saw me as weak. Vulnerable. Not perfect. And since I'm none of those things, you would leave me. Again."

There. The truth was out. Kate wondered if her world was about to crash down on her. Her shoulders sagged.

She stared at his hand linked with hers. "I get it. I'm not good enough. My company isn't important enough for you to stay."

"Oh, babe. Those aren't reasons for a person to leave."

His words made her want to cry. She blinked.

"But that's what always happened before." Her voice broke. "If I did something they didn't like, they sent me away."

His lips parted. "Your foster parents? They would send you away?"

Kate nodded, ashamed of not being enough for anyone. But she realized this was why she cut her losses so easily instead of fighting. She hadn't known, so she couldn't control the way she reacted. "Not every foster home was like that. There were some wonderful families—decent, caring people. The family Susan and I lived with during high school was great. Well, until they had to move out of state our senior year and were unable to take us with them, but we'd been accepted to college and were turning eighteen, so it wasn't so bad."

Jared squeezed her hand. "I had no idea."

His tenderness gave her courage, enabling her to continue. "Another family talked about adopting me when I was ten. They were nice, but the father lost his job, and the mother got pregnant and... I figured out if I could be perfect, everything would be okay. So I tried to be the perfect daughter, the perfect student, the perfect wife. But it wasn't enough for you."

His eyes softened. "Oh, Katie."

She didn't want his pity. She wanted his love.

"I thought I'd gotten over my past, but then you wanted to move to Seattle, and I didn't. You left anyway, and, well, history repeated itself.

Unfortunately, I wasn't perfect then, and I'm not perfect now." She looked at the blanket, feeling lost and alone. "I'm sorry I failed you."

Jared stared at his wife, stunned. He wanted to wipe away her fear and sadness. He wanted to make her smile and make her understand how much he loved her. Not for what she did or didn't do, but for who she was. Things she'd told him before made sense, enabling him to put the pieces together finally. Now, he had to make everything right.

"You're more than enough, sweetheart. After our second date, I told Brady you were a keeper. I only left because I was trying to force you to come with me. That was a horrible plan that backfired on me in the worst way." He rubbed his thumb over her skin. "You are Ms. Practical. Ms. Take Charge. Ms. Planner Extraordinaire. I admire those traits, but I love Kate, the whole package. I'm sorry I didn't dig deeper and learn more about you and what happened to you in the past better. But we have our entire lives ahead of us to discover each other."

Her wide eyes filled with wonder. "Our entire lives?"

"You're not getting rid of me that easy." His smile waned. "But I need to tell you something, too."

"You can tell me anything."

Jared hoped so. Years of living with strangers, many who didn't want her or wouldn't love her, had made Kate vulnerable. She might appear tough and stubborn, but those were ways to keep her heart from being broken again. He'd broken her heart, anyway. He'd hurt her. The same as the strangers she'd grown up with, but it wouldn't happen again.

Still, for them to move forward, they needed to face the past.

"My whole life, I've only cared about winning," he explained. "A video game, an argument, or our marriage. I didn't care as long as I came out on top. If we divorced, I would have been considered a failure." She stared up at him with her emotions so exposed Jared struggled to continue. "That's why I agreed to the marriage of convenience. That's why I took time off and came to Portland."

She swallowed. "And now?"

"I owe you an apology. A massive one." His eyes were wet, and he blinked. "I thought I loved you when I proposed and we got married. But that's nothing compared to my love for you now."

The love she needed. The love they both needed.

And Jared finally understood.

"The only thing I want, Katie. The only thing I need, is you."

He pulled her on to his lap, mindful of her head injury and IV cord, and brushed his lips across her nape.

"Before, I would leave for a week or more with no problem. I didn't like it, but I figured when our schedules meshed, we were meant to be together." He pushed a strand of hair off her face. "Now, I want to go to sleep with you by my side and wake up next to you every morning."

"In Seattle," she said, sounding resigned.

That *was* what he wanted, but that wasn't what Kate needed.

He'd grown up knowing whether he fought or argued or told his family off, things would be okay. His family gave him security, support, and love, no matter what. That was something she didn't have, but he would give that to her now.

Kate shouldn't have made all the sacrifices, uprooting her life and disrupting her career to live together when he wasn't even around during the week. He should have been the one to do that.

Not because she owned a company or he had more flexibility to work part-time, or a million other things. But because he was more secure than she was. Jared would give Kate what she needed because he loved her. Unconditionally. That love was more important than his job or winning or anything else.

"I did," he admitted. "But being in Seattle isn't the best thing for us."

"Us?"

"I want us to move back to Portland."

She inhaled sharply. "Your job?"

"My job is taking care of you and Cassidy. That's what I need to do. Maybe once we're settled, I'll look into working from home, consulting, or something new."

"But your family—"

"*You* are my family. You and Cassidy."

Her eyes darkened. "I don't want to alienate your parents."

"My mom and dad will be thrilled to have Cassidy closer. My dad can use his contacts to help me set up a business. And everyone is sorry for how they treated you."

"Really?"

The hope in her voice brought a smile to his face. "Really. But you need to promise we'll talk to each other. We'll communicate what's happening in our lives and our hearts no matter what. Our needs, our fears, our dreams—nothing will be off-limits."

Her smile lit up her face. "I promise."

"If we get into an argument or disagreement, nothing will change how I feel. I love you, Kate Malone." He embraced her, wanting them to be this close forever. "I will always love you."

"I love you, too."

"I have something for you." Jared pulled a familiar-looking navy-blue box from his jacket pocket. "I've been waiting for the perfect time—"

"There is no such thing as perfect."

He laughed. "Then now is as good a time as any."

She untied the blue and white ribbon and opened the top. Inside the box lay a pink heart charm with diamonds and white flowers on it. "So beautiful."

"Like you."

"Thank you." She removed the charm. "I love it. And you."

"My heart will always be with you." He clipped the charm onto her bracelet. "So be careful with it, okay?"

"I'll cherish your heart always." She held her arm with the bracelet to her chest. "And never break it. Deal?"

"Deal."

Jared sealed their bargain with a kiss. He had only meant to brush his lips against hers, but the way Kate rose to meet him sent his blood roaring through his veins. He couldn't get enough of her. Of her sweetness and her warmth. Need pulsated through him. He wanted her, but not here. Not now. There would be a lifetime of kisses ahead of them, so he drew the kiss to an end.

* * *

Wow. Kate tried to control her breathing.

What a kiss. What a man.

My man.

My husband.

"I never thought love could ever be like this." The smile on her lips matched the one in her heart. She'd never experienced such happiness. "I'm so glad I was wrong. I thought you were a dream come true for me, but we got married, and nothing changed. We still acted single, living our separate lives during the week and being together on weekends."

Jared kissed the top of her hand. "Be prepared for that to change."

She nodded.

"Since Cassidy came into our lives, I saw a new side to you." Joy bubbled inside Kate. "And I fell in love with you all over again. Only this time, the love was deeper, stronger. And this is only the beginning."

He lowered his mouth to hers, his lips soft and gentle. His kiss made her feel special, beautiful, alive. She soaked up the essence of the man he was. The man who showed her how amazing love could be. As his heartbeat thundered against her chest, Kate smiled. Nothing had ever felt so right.

"You've taught me to trust, Jared." His affection for her shone in his eyes and sent a warm glow pulsing through her. "Not only you but also my heart. And my heart keeps screaming over and over again, how much I love you."

"I love you, too."

She relished in the pleasure his words brought. "I want to be with you. I want to be married to you. And Cassidy needs a brother or sister. Or both."

His dimpled smile reached his eyes. "No argument here. I agree on all counts."

"It won't be easy being parents or having a successful marriage. But we will make it work."

"We."

Not I. "Yes, we."

She and Jared were meant to be together as Susan had written in her letter. Their love would help them overcome whatever came their way—good or bad. They would succeed for Cassidy and each other.

Kate pressed her lips against his. Forget caffeine. This was the only jolt she needed. As he pulled her closer, she went eagerly, her mouth moving over his, taking all he had to give. In his arms, she'd found security and strength, peace and happiness, love and a family. She wanted it all; she wanted him. Today. Tomorrow. Forever.

Jared pulled back. "You're wrong about one thing, though."

"What's that?"

"I know something perfect."

Her eyes widened. "What?"

"You." He kissed the top of her hand with all the chivalry of a knight from so long ago. "You're perfect for me."

Epilogue

A year later…

Friday evening, Kate pulled into the driveway, ready to put the week behind her. Oh, it had gone well. They had a full roster of clients, so she planned on hiring additional people so they could take on more work. But now, she wanted to forget about everything except Jared and Cassidy. For the next three days—Mondays were an official day off for her—she would focus only on her family and herself.

She removed the keys from the ignition, grabbed her laptop bag, and slid from the car. No lights were on downstairs, but that wasn't surprising. Since they remodeled—taking the house down to its studs and foundation—Jared and Cassidy spent more time upstairs in the bonus room, aka the playroom.

The door was unlocked, so Kate dropped her keys into her purse and stepped inside. Dark and empty. She flicked on the light switch and set her bag on the entryway table. The usual smell of dinner cooking was missing, too. A peek in the kitchen showed no pots or pans on the stove. That must mean they were eating out. Good, because that meant less cleanup for them later. She was ready to have some fun.

After kicking off her heels, she headed up the stairs. The playroom's door was closed. That was odd.

"Jared," she called out.

"In here," he answered from inside the bonus room.

Kate opened the door.

"Surprise!" voices shouted.

Kate did a double take. He held Cassidy, but others were there too. Frank and Margery. Heather, Hannah, Sam, Tucker, their spouses, and kids. A handful of people from her office were also present: Sean, Maisie, and Emily, who was back from her maternity leave and now working as the managing director to relieve some of Kate's responsibilities.

"What's going on?" Balloons covered the ceiling. A buffet table was set up in a corner—drinks in another. There were even presents wrapped in bright paper and tied with ribbons. "It's not my birthday. Or Cassidy's. I know I didn't forget our anniversary."

"You didn't, but it's been one year since we moved home from Seattle. You were recovering from a concussion, so it's okay you don't remember the date."

"Well, I'm shocked," Sean chimed in. "Because Kate forgets nothing."

Everyone laughed.

With a beaming smile, Jared came toward her. He placed a small box in Cassidy's hand. "Give that to your mommy."

The baby who seemed to grow bigger each day handed it to Kate. "Mama."

"Yes." Jared kissed the little one's head. "It's for your mama, and she should open it."

Kate did and then held up the pink kitty wearing a diamond bow charm. "Oh, I love it so much. I've always wanted a cat. The charm will look fantastic on my bracelet. Thank you so much, but I don't understand why there's a party."

"It's a mommy shower," Hannah announced with an enormous grin.

Heather nodded. "We, as in my sister and brothers, did this because you never got a bridal shower before you married Jared or a baby shower when Cassidy arrived."

"A little late," Hannah said. "But better than never."

Tucker held up his hands. "In full disclosure, I only bought the drinks and picked up the dessert. Dad took care of the catering."

A lump of emotion clogged Kate's throat. Jared's family had tried to make up for what they'd done last Mother's Day and before that even. But she had never expected this. She swallowed. "Thanks."

"Let's eat before the food gets cold." Frank motioned to the buffet table. "Then, we can give Kate her presents."

Margery hugged her. "You're the guest of honor, so you get to go first."

"Come on, babe." As Jared held Cassidy with one arm, he placed his hand at the small of Kate's back and led her to the food, which was a mix of Thai, Indian, pizza, and pub food. "My dad asked for a list of your favorite takeout. I guess he couldn't pick just one."

She leaned against him and touched Cassidy. "I-I don't know what to say."

Jared kissed Kate. "Words aren't necessary. This must be overwhelming."

"A complete shock."

"You deserve it." He kissed her again. "And so much more."

Even though people were eating, the noise level rose. The food was delicious, and Kate felt feted like a queen. After dinner, she opened gifts, receiving a spa gift card, face mask set, fuzzy socks, and other small pampering items. "Thank you. I appreciate all of you doing this. I can't tell you what it means. I'm so happy to be a part of the Reed family."

His siblings beamed, and his parents exchanged a glance.

Cassidy toddled to Maisie and hugged her.

"The night's not over yet." Jared stood. "I'll be right back."

"More gifts," one of Kate's nieces announced. "Those are the best part of a party."

Kate smiled at her. "Having everyone here and the cake is good, too."

"Close your eyes," he said.

She did.

Someone gasped, and a kid squealed. But Kate kept her eyes shut.

"You can open them now," Jared said.

He held a gray kitten with the greenest of eyes. "This is your other gift from Cassidy and me."

Kate inhaled sharply. "It matches the charm."

"The cat came first," he teased. "Cassidy picked her out. I hope you don't mind."

"This is perfect." Kate cuddled the kitten. "She's adorable."

"Like her sister and her mom," Jared said.

"I love her." And Kate already did. "Does she have a name?"

"Not yet." Jared rubbed under the kitten's chin, and she purred like a generator. "What do you want to call her?"

As she considered ideas, her family suggested names.

"Silver."

"Cat."

"Francesca."

"Kitty."

Cassidy ran to them. "Cat."

"Yes, sweetie." Kate helped her daughter pet the kitten. "What should we name her?"

Cassidy tilted her head and stared at the ceiling. "A-gel."

Jared looked at Kate. "I've never heard her say that before."

"Me, either, but it's a fitting name for such a sweet kitten." Kate held up the ball of fur. "Everyone, meet Angel."

The kitten soon fell asleep, leaving Cassidy to take center stage, and Kate was happy to let them bask in the spotlight. She sat with Jared and the cat. "Thank you."

"My family did all the work."

Kate glanced at the sleeping kitten on her lap. "Did they buy my charm and cat?"

"No."

"Then, thank you." She kissed him, a slow, hot kiss she'd wanted to give him all evening. "Especially for the newest member of the Reed clan."

"I figured it was time."

"It was." Kate and Jared had almost lost something precious, but what they'd overcome had only made their marriage stronger. She gazed into his eyes. "I love you."

"Love you."

As he kissed her, Kate's heart filled with joy.

Jared drew back. "We're just getting started."

"I know." And she did.

One day—Kate hoped that would be sooner rather than later—they would add more members.

A dog, for sure. Maybe another cat.

And children. It wouldn't matter whether the kids were biological, foster, adopted, or a combination of the three. She couldn't wait to see how her and Jared's family would grow.

The kitten woke and meowed, so she held Angel against her chest. "You're fine, little one. We'll take wonderful care of you."

As Angel's eyes closed again, words from Susan's letter popped into Kate's mind.

I want Cassidy to experience what being part of a loving family is all about. Jared with the crazy, meddlesome Reeds can provide that for her. She can have what we didn't have growing up. I need that for my child. Take care of my baby and love her the way we wanted to be loved!

Kate stared at Cassidy, love overflowing for her daughter, who was the perfect combination of Susan and Brady. "We are."

* * * * * *

If you'd like to read the next book in the A Keeper Series, ***The Date: An Online Dating Romance***, you can find it here: https://melissamcclone.com/Date.

One tech entrepreneur, one blond bombshell, and two rival dating sites...

When Dani Bennett lands a new marketing job, she can't wait to prove herself. But her excitement fizzles when her new boss insists she create an online dating profile to spy on the competition. Quitting isn't an option; she needs the money. Now, she must meet the charming guy who's been messaging her. Dani, however, has played this game before. She knows exactly what he's after—what they're all after. It's a good thing she has a foolproof plan to keep her date from being interested in her.

Bryce Delaney works hard to keep scammers from infiltrating his dating website. He'll do anything to keep his clients and his company safe, like asking a potential corporate spy to meet him for coffee. When the woman turns out to be more hobo than hottie, he's intrigued. She has no idea he founded the dating website, and he plans to keep it that way until he can uncover her agenda.

As one date leads to another, sparks fly. Dani knows a relationship built on lies will never work, but she's not the only one with a secret. Will the truth bring her and Bryce closer or send them back online to find someone else to love?

About the Author

USA Today bestselling author Melissa McClone has written over forty-five sweet contemporary romance novels. She lives in the Pacific Northwest with her husband, three children, a spoiled Norwegian Elkhound, and cats who think they rule the house. They do!

If you'd like to find Melissa online:
www.melissamcclone.com
www.facebook.com/melissamcclonebooks
www.facebook.com/groups/McCloneTroopers
twitter.com/melissamcclone
www.instagram.com/melmcclone